DESTINY'S JOURNEY

The Adventure Continues

DJ Steel

ChiVaree

A catalogue record for this book is available from the National Library of Australia

ISBN: 978-0-9944086-3-1 (paperback)
ISBN: 978-0-9944086-4-8 (ebook)
ISBN 978-0-9944086-5-5 (hardcover)
Interior and Cover Illustrations: Christopher Brunton
Publisher: Chivaree Publishing
Book Cover Design: Christopher Brunton
Interior Design and Cover Formatting: Pickawoowoo Publishing Group
Print and Channel Distribution: Lightning Source / Ingram (US/UK/AUS/ EUR)

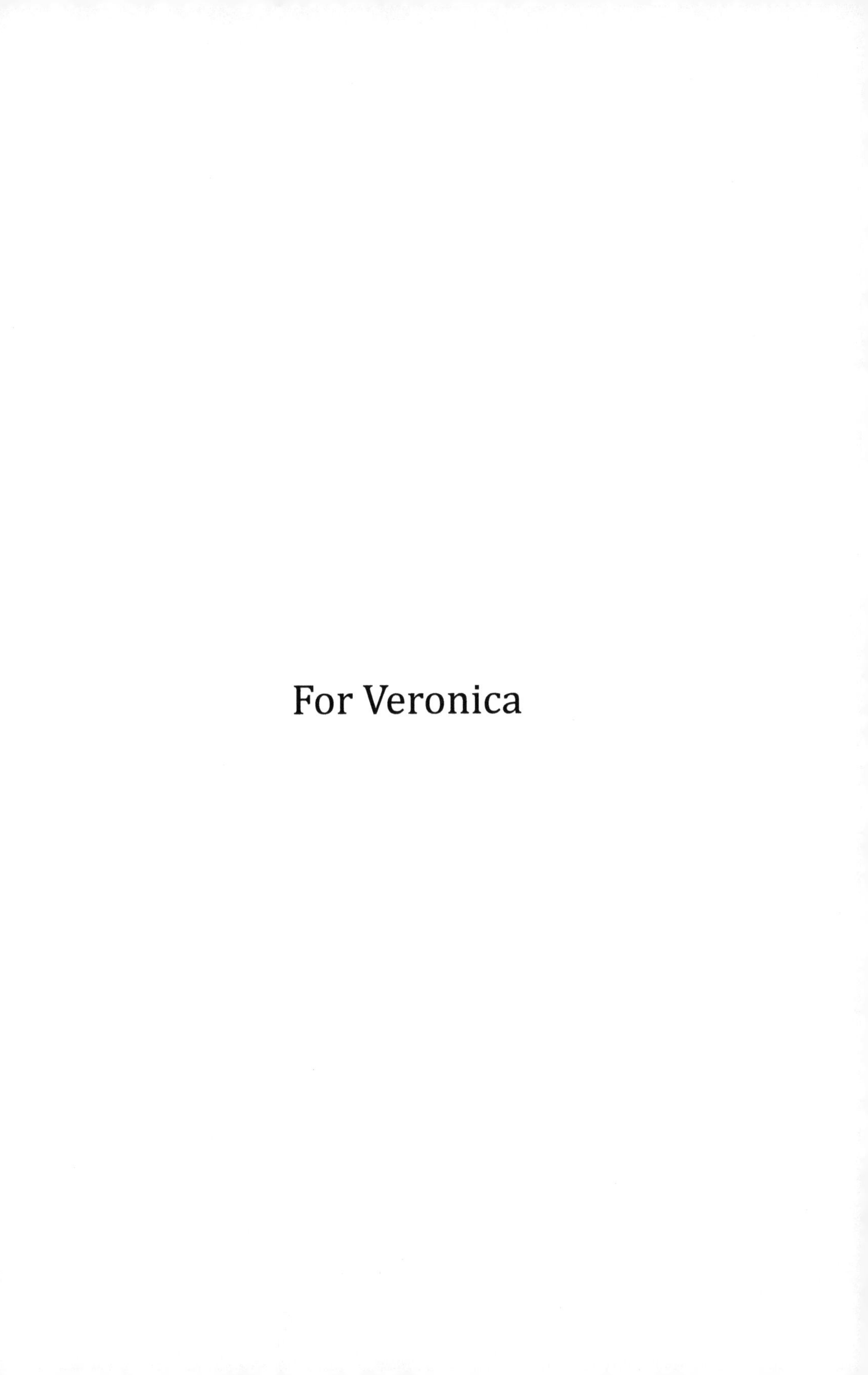

For Veronica

Hilltopia
Hilltopia Harbour
Kleeveden Bay
Savo Island
Hermanstock Island
Penstown
Peagreen Sea
Little Havoc
The Great Quay
Benaback
Angarrad
Brunton

Contents

Chapter 1   Shonky is rescued 1

Chapter 2   The adoption proposal 17

Chapter 3   The dream begins 29

Chapter 4   The sea beckons 37

Chapter 5   The island that has no name 47

Chapter 6   The Great Quay 57

Chapter 7   Maximum Mischief sets sail 67

Chapter 8   Mischief visits Little Havoc 75

Chapter 9   The fleets assemble 83

Chapter 10 An ill omen 93

Chapter 11 The great sea battle 101

Chapter 12 Burial at sea 111

Chapter 13 The adoption party 121

The Story So Far ...

In a previous encounter, Destiny Drummond, a 12-year-old girl who has lost both her parents in an horrific car crash is left unable to use her legs, trapped in a wheelchair. She is on a quest to find all the remaining members of her family.

In the care of foster parents, Anita Hargreaves and her mother Anne, Destiny falls ill and is taken to hospital with a fever. During the three days she is unconscious in hospital, she is whisked away to the dream world.

She encounters Angelique, a beautiful woman who reveals herself as Destiny's Dream Guardian. She then meets twin brothers Manky and Shonky, the mysterious gentleman called Count Dabacus and lastly but not least, Buttondrop the Maptoodoo, the Wish-Master. A trip to the Crumpled Faced People's sacred island is also a highlight.

Kidnapped by Maximum Mischief at the county fair and locked up in his dungeon, Destiny and the twins are rescued by an unlikely friend, Jack, one of Mischief's servants. They escape and are pursued by Mischief's minions.

As they flee, they lose Shonky who falls into a raging river and disappears.

They are eventually reunited with their friends and protectors, and Destiny is readied to return to her real world. Waking up from her fever-induced dream, she excitedly tells her foster carers of her experiences. They look at her in wonder.

Now her adventure continues.

The last thing Destiny remembered was at the cliff edge as Shonky desperately held on for dear life. The river raged below.

"Don't fall!" Destiny cried.

"Hold on, I've got you," Jack shouted, fighting to be heard above the roaring waters.

Shonky held on to an exposed branch at the edge of the cliff with one hand and with the other, reached for Jack's outstretched hand.

"I'm slipping," he cried.

"No!" yelled Manky, his brother.

Shonky's small hands began to lose their grip. He just couldn't keep holding. He fell. The river below rushed madly in its eagerness to empty into the open sea.

Shonky was swept on by the uncaring, raging current. He struggled furiously, choking on all the water he was swallowing. His head disappeared beneath the swirling, hungry torrent, his vision obscured by the murky mud-coloured water as he was taken onward down the stream. Desperately, he mustered all the strength in his body to keep his head above water but the relentless might of the river kept pulling him under.

"He's gone," Jack said quietly.

"Oh, my brother," Manky sobbed.

"He may still be all right," said Destiny, refusing to give in to the tears welling in her eyes.

"We'll climb down."

"No, the cliff is too steep. Look at the rocks," Jack said.

Below them, vicious, jagged rocks jutted up from the treacherous waters like cruel talons. The wind whipped and whistled through them and the roar was deafening.

Quietly, Destiny, Jack and Manky sat at the edge of cliff.

"Oh, my stupid brother," Manky sobbed.

The three sat closely together and put their arms around each other. The sun hung low in the sky. Night was approaching.

"We must keep moving," Jack said. "Maximum Mischief's men are not far behind. We have to get to Angelique's place before it gets dark." Angelique was Destiny's Dream Guardian who was tasked with guiding Destiny while she was in the dream world.

"We can't leave Shonky behind," Destiny said, finally giving way to the tears as they streamed down her sad face.

"There's nothing we can do for him now. Come on," Jack implored.

The three slowly rose but lingered a little longer. They hugged each other. The river below raged and the sun hung lower on the horizon like a darkening copper disc. A brisk breeze blew through their hair and clothes. Solemn and in silence, they resumed their trek.

Further down the way, Maximum Mischief's minions were in hot pursuit.

"I can smell them," one of them snarled with gleeful malice. "We're getting close," the minions chorused bloodily with the thought of capturing their prey.

It was Maximum Mischief, the local menace, who had kidnapped Destiny, Manky and Shonky and locked them up in his dungeon. Brave young Jack had freed them and now they were running for their lives.

While she was in hospital with a urinary infection, Destiny Drummond, a 12-year-old girl in a wheelchair in the real world, had fallen into a restless fever and was now in the dreamscape.

Many calamities had befallen her but she had the protection of the Wish-Master, Buttondrop the Maptoodoo, her Dream Guardian, Angelique, the mysterious Count Dabacus and now her new-found friends Manky, Shonky and Jack.

Destiny was devastated by Shonky's fall as he disappeared beneath the treacherous waters. Despite all the arguments she tried to put together in her mind, it seemed indeed there was nothing they could do to save him. Sadly, Destiny remembered the twin brothers Manky and Shonky who had befriended her in Hilltopia. She scolded herself for having a happy memory, however this seemed to make her all the more heartbroken.

Manky, Jack and Destiny picked up their pace and headed for Hilltopia where they knew Buttondrop, Angelique and Count Dabacus were waiting for them. The friendly lights on the horizon told them that safety was close by as they stumbled onward. They reached the outskirts of town where they met a party of townsfolk armed with pitchforks and lanterns with their beloved Buttondrop.

"Thank God you are safe. Come quickly, we must get you to shelter," Buttondrop said, checking them for any injuries. He bundled them up in warm blankets and guided them to sanctuary.

Back in the river, Shonky struggled with the fast current. *I must keep my head above water and go with the flow,* he thought. Swiftly it carried him on, down past the sharp boulders into a wide, open stream. *I must try to reach the bank.* On and on the river swept him as his strength began to fade. *I must be brave,* he said to himself.

He decided to lie on his back and let the mighty river carry him wherever it wanted. He concentrated on his breathing and managed to stay afloat. He looked at the stars above him in a clear sky. He stayed calm. He heard a loud roar and realised he was approaching the mouth of the river. A barrage of breakers buffeted and tossed him like a rag doll. He swallowed a mouthful of salt water but managed to get past them, swimming as furiously as he could.

He was now in the open sea. All went quiet.

Shonky drifted and was able to avoid swallowing more salt water. He was tired. The night seemed to last an eternity as he floated and tried not to fall asleep. It was impossible – his eyes would close and he would swallow more of the hideous salt water. His mind began to wander and he thought of his brother Manky, Destiny and Jack, and he heard Angelique call his name. He became confused and disorientated. In spite of the foul water, it was in fact keeping him afloat: maybe he wasn't so bad off after all? The first rays of the new morning began to appear. He closed his eyes and kept his mind on staying relaxed.

Time seemed to stand still, and despite his best efforts Shonky fell into an exhausted sleep. Splash! The sound of paddles in the water alerted him and he opened his eyes to see a boat.

"What kind of fish have we got here?" he heard a man's voice say kindly.

A grappling hook reached out and caught onto Shonky's collar. He felt himself being dragged into a rowing boat by many pairs of hands.

"Where did you come from?" a fisherman asked.

Shonky was too tired to speak as he lay on the bottom of the boat. The fishermen resumed their rowing and headed back to the mother ship, a trawler. They lifted him aboard gently.

"Quiet now," one of the fishermen said. "You're safe now."

The captain of the ship was called. Shonky heard the men talking but he was not able to work out what they were saying. He felt a spoon at his mouth and hungrily took in the porridge offered. It was delicious.

"Slowly," a voice said.

The sea was calm as the fishermen attended to Shonky. Nets were strewn across the deck together with various grappling hooks and other seagoing implements. Seagulls rested on top of the ship and on the rails. The smell of brine was strong in the air and the warmth of the morning sun kept a slight chill at bay.

"Get this one to a bunk, he needs rest," the captain ordered.

Tucking him into bed, the fishermen left Shonky. He laid on his back with his eyes on the ceiling for a while until a peaceful sleep overtook him. He began dreaming. Faces he didn't recognise peered at him and he tossed and turned. Voices called out to him but he couldn't make out what they were saying. He saw planets and stars and felt as if he was floating among them. He wandered through swirling clouds of coloured gas, nebulae. And then there was darkness and silence.

The fishermen discussed their find and were full of wonder at how he managed to survive. They had seen many strange things on their voyages at sea but this took the cake. The captain checked the ship's status with his crew. The storerooms were full of frozen fish and they had all they could store. He ordered the ship home to the safe haven of Hilltopia's harbour.

The engines, that had been idling, were revved and the captain set course for port.

Hilltopia Harbour was full of ships and boats as the captain manoeuvred the trawler to its mooring and the crew brought out the thick hemp ropes to secure the boat. Bustling shore workers climbed up gangways and unloaded the splendid haul of fish. Busy hands grabbed nets to be mended. Ropes were wound around sturdy capstans and tied off. Shonky continued to sleep as the fishermen spread the word around about their find. News travelled fast and soon the whole town was talking about this strange happening.

The men from the fishing boat were quizzed about their unusual find. How did you find him? Who is he? Is he safe now? What will happen to him now, this strange boy found floating in the open sea?

A deeply sad Angelique was at the shopping centre when she overheard two women talking about it at the checkout. She had almost given up hope that Shonky had survived the river fall, however there was a nagging feeling she could not put aside that somehow he was able to reach safety. Her gift of vision and her psychic abilities were clouded and she was not able to determine what had happened to him. Although the town authorities were alerted to his disappearance and emergency workers were sent out in search parties, no trace of Shonky had been found.

Sidling up closer to the talking women without trying to be too obvious, she heard of the strange fish found by fishermen in the ocean, a boy. The checkout girl rang up her purchases on a wooden cash register making a ringing sound with each entry. Angelique gave the girl her money which was placed in a cylinder overhead connected to the cashier's office by a series of cables. She received her change and charged out of the shop doors, ecstatic at the thought it could be Shonky. *Could it be him?* she thought excitedly, forgetting the groceries. Called back to the store, she gathered her goods packed in brown paper bags and apologised for her forgetfulness.

Exhausted, her heart racing and catching her breath, she placed her shopping bags on the kitchen table and called Manky from his room. He had been staying with Angelique since escaping Maximum Mischief's clutches.

He hadn't wandered out in days and she was worried about him.

"You won't believe what I've just heard," she said to him. "Sit down and I'll make us a nice cup of tea."

"What is it?" Manky said dejectedly.

"A fishing trawler out in the ocean found a young boy floating alone. Incredible. They fished him out and he is with them now at the harbour. Apparently, he has lost his memory and doesn't know who is. Oh, could it be him, Manky?" she said sadly.

"No, Shonky is lost for good," Manky said.

"No, we must investigate," Angelique said sternly.

"I'll put this shopping away and you go and hitch up Toby and the carriage. I'll be right with you."

Manky headed for the barn and went through the motions of getting the carriage ready. He started to think. *No, surely not. It couldn't possibly be. Shonky is gone. There's no point holding on to false hopes. I saw him go under, I'm sure. Oh, my precious brother, why did things have to happen this way?* He put it out of his mind. *We'll see,* he thought.

The trip into town seemed to take forever. Manky kept silent as Angelique held the reins guiding Toby the horse along the unsealed dirt road. Approaching the centre of Hilltopia, pretty wooden cottages with thatched roofs lined the streets as they wound their way to the harbour.

Hilltopia was an old village, steeped in history. Its founder was an adventurer named Thomas Hinchcliffe, who established a community and brought in many relatives and friends to start a settlement. The thriving town was now the supply centre for the many farmers who came to tend the rich volcanic soils of the surrounding district. Fields of wheat, oats and barley, and shepherds with their flocks of cattle, sheep, pigs and goats were now a staple of the area.

Hinchcliffe had built a pipeline from the nearby river to secure the town's water supply. Farmers also used the river to irrigate their fields. The townspeople had to be on their guard, though. Many times the scurrilous Maximum Mischief tried to sabotage their supply but they held him in check.

The dastardly plan was to rupture the pipeline in several places, quite a distance from each other, and at the same time disable the waterwheel that drew up the precious liquid into the large pipeline. The plan was foiled, however, by alert workers.

Angelique and Manky arrived at the harbour. They went to the main office and inquired about the boy who was found at sea.

A young woman named Sally at the reception desk excitedly told them the whole story.

"Such a miracle," she said. "He has lost his memory and doesn't know who he is or where he is. Do you know who he is? The whole town is talking about this strange event. Are you relatives? Was he washed out to sea? So many unanswered questions! Oh, what a story I'll have to tell the family tonight," Sally gushed.

"We might have a clue to his identity," Angelique said.

"Just one moment and I will call the harbour sheriff. If you can identify him, the sheriff will release him into your custody," Sally said.

Manky brought out his wallet and showed the young woman a dog-eared, sepia photograph of himself and Shonky.

"Yes, that's him all right. Just a second," she said.

The sheriff arrived and negotiated with Manky and Angelique. They told him the whole story of being kidnapped and imprisoned and the escape. They explained about his fall from the cliff while being pursued. The sheriff, very gravely, took this all into account.

"He's lucky to be alive, in that case," he said.

"Come on, I'll show you where he is," he said, leading them to the trawler which had picked up Shonky.

The captain of the ship met them on the deck.

"The boy is still sleeping," he said. "Do you want me to wake him up?"

"No, just let me take a look at him," Manky said.

And there he was, sound asleep, as snug as a bug in a rug on the bunk below deck. Manky and Angelique watched him quietly and cried. It was him, Shonky.

"He looks so peaceful," Angelique whispered.

Shonky opened his eyes. He looked at the strangers before him and wondered who they were.

"Shonky, it's me, your brother Manky."

Shonky looked at him puzzled and confused but said nothing.

"Me too, Shonky, it's Angelique."

Shonky just smiled.

"You're coming home with us until your memory comes back," Manky said.

The sheriff and captain took Shonky aside and asked him if he understood what was happening. Shonky, for his part, felt a bit confused and bewildered but had a good feeling about these people. He couldn't explain it but he felt safe with them. He told the two men.

"That's settled," the sheriff said, smiling. "Take better care of yourself, young man."

"We'll take him to the hospital first to check him out," Angelique said. "He will recuperate at my house. Here is my card should you wish to contact me. Thank you so much for all your kindness. I will keep you posted of his progress."

Turning to the brothers, Angelique said: "It's almost lunchtime. I have a wonderful idea. Ricotta cheese and spinach pie and fresh, crispy salad. I have all the ingredients. You must be so hungry, Shonky! Do you mind me calling you that?" she said coyly.

Shonky just smiled.

Off they set for home.

What they didn't know, though, was that they were being watched closely. A scruffy young boy with buck teeth and red hair had been observing the whole encounter. He was one of Maximum Mischief's spies instructed to watch the comings and goings at the harbour. He smirked.

Ha, gotcha, he said to himself. He hurried back to Mischief's keep and told Clotilda the witch the whole story. Clotilda smacked her lips.

"Good, master will be pleased," she said. "Off with you!"

Clotilda, a most hated and feared woman, was a devoted servant of her master, Maximum Mischief. She, together with the club-footed Rankle, looked after the everyday affairs at the dark castle and they ran a tight ship.

Clotilda felt smug. *Well, well, well, won't he be pleased*, she thought.

Winding her way to Maximum Mischief's study, the stairs groaned as she passed niches in the wall where gargoyle heads with eyes that glowed menacingly watched. Stopping to stroke each head, she cooed their names one by one. She knocked nervously on the door.

"Go away, I'm busy," Mischief shouted.

"But Master, I have some important news," she offered, using her best snivelling voice.

"Enter."

Clotilda went in and approached the desk.

"Hurry up, I haven't got all day," he snarled.

She ran her finger along the desktop as the news unfolded. Mischief fumed. *Familiar,* he said to himself. *I shall soon drive that out of her.*

"Upstarts!" he said. "I'll soon fix them. Send out the men, burn down the house, capture the three of them and bring them to me," he ordered.

Clotilda left quickly and gave orders to Maximum Mischief's minions who were lazing about in the giant courtyard in the grounds of the castle. Some were cutting their toenails, some were picking their noses while others practised their roping skills, throwing lassos at a pillar situated in the middle of the grounds. Still some played cards and drank beer but they all jumped to attention when Clotilda appeared.

Not knowing the fate awaiting them, Angelique and Manky were getting Shonky settled. They pulled out some old photographs of themselves together wearing big grins and looking very happy and showed them to him. Shonky didn't respond. It was late in the afternoon but night soon fell and the three retired to their bedrooms.

Under cover of darkness, the minions located Angelique's house and scouted around. Their dark clothes melded in with the darkness of the night making them just shadowy figures. Only the gentle light from the two moons lit the way. Knowing their deadly task, they silently started a number of fires around the house and retreated to cover across the road to watch their foul deed unfold.

"What's that smell? I can smell something burning," Manky shouted, alerting the others.

"Fire!" Shonky yelled.

Manky ran outside and was horrified to find the house well ablaze. He bolted back inside and told the others what was happening.

"Quick, we must leave before we are overcome by smoke," Angelique shouted. "Help me with the animals, we must get them to safety." They rushed outside to the barn, released the hens and roosters, took Toby out of his stall and gathered the cat and dog. By this time the blaze had taken well hold and flames leaped up into the night sky, creating an eerie light.

Neighbours came out of their homes and gathered on the footpath outside the flaming inferno. The fire brigade was alerted and soon arrived with bells ringing. The minions remained hidden. They snickered and wrestled with each other in delight as the tragedy unfolded.

"Keep all the animals together," Angelique said. "We head for the church where we can take shelter. Leave everything else behind."

Off set the unlikely group, headed for the centre of town. Manky and Shonky kept the gathering together as Angelique led the way. Father Primus, the local rector, met them at the doors of the church. He had heard the bells of the fire brigade passing and had come over from the rectory, where he lived, to investigate.

"Goodness gracious me, what is all this?" he said.

"Oh Father, my house is on fire. We need shelter," Angelique cried.

Father Primus became very serious and ushered the group into the main hall.

The minions were in hot pursuit but baulked when the group reached the church and backed off. Regrouping, they discussed their next move. Taking a shortcut through some vacant land, they planned to cut off the fleeing companions from their escape route. However, Angelique and company had anticipated a trap and themselves had taken a shortcut to reach shelter.

"Clotilda is going to whip us for this," one of the minions said, fearfully. They headed off back to the castle with bowed heads.

Father Primus made tea for everyone and made sure they were settled. His housekeeper, Mrs Warboys, woken by all the commotion, busied herself in the kitchen making refreshments. The friends tended to each other as best they could, their eyes stinging and their lungs burning.

"What do we do now, Angelique?" Manky asked despondently. He shook his head trying to take in everything that had happened.

"I must get in touch with Buttondrop," she said with a grim face. He was her mentor and good friend, always a great help in a stoush. Buttondrop would know what to do.

Settling into an armchair, Angelique closed her eyes and inclined her head slightly.

"What's she doing?" Shonky said quietly.

"Ssshhh, she is using mental telepathy. She can send messages through her mind. She is trying to contact Buttondrop. Be very quiet for a while," Manky said. The brothers watched her intently as she rested her hands on the armchair. After a while, with eyes still closed, she began to smile a gentle smile.

Manky smiled too. He knew she had made contact.

"I have contacted Count Dabacus too. They will be here soon. Let's rest now. After a good night's sleep we will worry about things tomorrow," Angelique said. Count Dabacus was another friend who had much wisdom and experience in tight situations. The three of them had teamed up many times over the years with their work helping others realise their potential.

Father Primus prepared bedding and blankets and bade them all a good night. Mrs Warboys assisted then retired to her room.

Outside the two moons shone brightly in the night sky and all was quiet. The three settled in for the night and were soon fast asleep. All was as well as could be.

THE ADOPTION PROPOSAL

Destiny was excited. While her foster grandmother Anne was taking her to school, she told the young girl that there was a big surprise for her when she got home.

"Oh, tell me what it is. Tell me now, Grandma!" Destiny pleaded.

"No, you will have to wait. Your Mum will let you know this afternoon. First things first, young lady, you have the day at school to worry about."

Anne got the wheelchair out of the back of the van and helped Destiny settle. Destiny's best friend Sarah came bounding up to greet them.

"Random!" she declared, shining a big smile on them both. "Did you hear about Lisa Markwell? She was caught sneaking out of her bedroom the other night and got into

BIG trouble with her parents. She's not at school today. Her parents let the teachers know what happened. Boy, is she in deep doo doo."

"Goodness gracious, Sarah, where do you get all this stuff from?" Anne smiled.

"I keep my eyes peeled and my ears tuned, Mrs Hargreaves. You gotta keep on top of things, you know. Never know what will happen next," Sarah boasted.

"Silly head," Destiny said with a frown.

"Blah, blah, blah," Sarah retorted lightheartedly.

Taking the handles, Sarah pushed Destiny towards the school buildings. Destiny turned back to wave goodbye to her Grandma. The school bell went off and the children began moving indoors.

"Who's up first today, Sarah?" Destiny asked.

"Mr Jurgens and religion studies. Come on. Do you have a music lesson today?"

"Yes, after lunch," Destiny replied.

"Yum, Mum packed me a big lunch today. A big yellow banana, tuna and lettuce sandwich, apple juice and a small packet of cheesy bite snacks. Can't wait," Sarah said with relish.

The children filed into the various classrooms to prepare for a day of learning.

"All right ladies and gents, settle down," Mr Jurgens said in a stern voice.

"This morning, we will be looking at one of the major religions of the world, Christianity. Can anyone tell me something about our subject?"

The whole class shot up their hands.

"Yes, Melissa, you go first. Please stand."

"Jesus is the Son of Man, the son of the Heavenly Father, who came to Earth to teach us," she said.

"Very good. You may sit. However, today we are going to concentrate on the historical Jesus, the Jewish man who lived some 2000 years ago. Can anyone tell me his historical name?"

The class was silent.

"His name was Yeshua and he lived in Galilee which is now today part of the modern nation of Israel in the Middle East. The language they spoke at the time was called Aramaic. There are many legends about this man, some of which have survived. He lived during the time of the Roman occupation. Rome held a tight reign over most of Europe."

A young girl put up her hand.

"Yes," Mr Jurgens said.

"My big sister read a book that said Jesus was married and had children."

"That's a lie," a boy said.

"Okay," Mr Jurgens interrupted. "It is true that Jewish men who lived in the time of Yeshua were expected to marry. However, as I said, much of what we know of the man himself has been lost in time. We only have what was written about him many years after his death, including the Bible."

"We keep a Bible in the house," a girl said.

"Yes, and we go to church. Just now and then, not all the time," another said.

"I saw a documentary on TV that said he was the most important man in human history," a boy said.

"Yes, he certainly set the world on fire," Mr Jurgens said. "Now, look at your computers. I have prepared some reading for you. Get busy."

The class proceeded to do this when a boy stood up from his desk and stood quietly.

"Yes, Mr Bass, what is it?"

"Jesus Christ is the only Begotten Son of the Father. He will come again to judge the living and the dead," he said softly.

Mr Jurgens smiled.

"All right, back to it," he said.

The room went quiet. Destiny saw something out of the corner of her eye and turned to look. A boy passed a note to a girl. She read it and her mouth dropped open and scowled at the author who was smirking. Destiny smiled gently and thought of Jack in the dreamworld. *I wonder what he is doing right now,* she thought. Her mind wandered. *What could Mum be up to? She has got something to tell me. I can't figure out what it might be.* She stared into space.

"Destiny Drummond, pay attention," Mr Jurgens cautioned.

"Sorry, Mr Jurgens," she said politely.

The lunch bell sounded. Sarah and Destiny sat together in the open school auditorium and enjoyed the tasty morsels their mothers had prepared. The sound of children chattering made quite a din. The supervising teachers wandered around keeping things in order. One little girl was crying by herself. A teacher went up to her.

"What's the matter Katrina?"

"I have no lunch."

"Mmmm. We can fix that. Wait one moment."

The teacher left but soon returned.

"Your mother left some money at the office for your lunch. Here, go to the tuckshop and buy whatever you like. Go on."

The girl cheered up and skipped away.

Destiny and Sarah looked at each other. They knew Katrina was often without her lunch and sometimes shared theirs with her.

Lunch finished, the children went to their next lessons. Sarah wheeled Destiny to her music lesson and told her she would catch up with her after school.

"Okay *mein kinder*, today we are going to look at a clarinet solo by the American composer George Gershwin, from the piece of music called "Rhapsody in Blue," the music teacher Mrs MacNamara said.

"Very jazzy!" she added and made a little wiggle which made the class burst into laughter.

"We will just listen and see what wonderful sounds the clarinet can make. Make yourselves comfortable. You can sit on the floor if you want. Here we go!"

The sound of music filled the room and the students listened intently. Mrs MacNamara stood at the front waving her hand to the beautiful strains. Destiny was awestruck. *That's too hard for me,* she thought. Destiny had chosen the clarinet as her favourite instrument and had been learning to play it for a few years now. She let the music wash over her and felt relaxed. *I can't wait to find out what Mum has to say.* And then, she remembered her real father playing something by Vivaldi, *The Four Seasons*, which made her sad. She bowed her head and closed her eyes, letting the beautiful music whisk her away as she thought of her parents and how much she missed them. Her reverie lasted only for short while, interrupted by the school bell.

"We're finished, little ones," Mrs MacNamara said with a big grin.

The children trundled out the classrooms and gathered their school bags. Sarah, brushing her mousy brown hair out of the way, rushed to meet Destiny. Her sharp, grey eyes soon spotted her prey. She pounced on Destiny like a cat.

"I'm out of here!" she said, exasperated.

"You're so silly, sometimes!" Destiny laughed.

Grandma Anne was in her usual parking spot, waiting for Destiny.

"Are you all right to get home, Sarah?" she asked.

"Yes. Dad's picking me up today. He shouldn't be too far away."

"Good. Do you want us to wait until he gets here?" Anne said.

"Oh, that would be nice, Mrs Hargreaves, thank you."

The sound of bustling cars and children filled the air as parents came to collect their rowdy charges. It wasn't long before Mr Santoro arrived.

"Bye! See you tomorrow," Sarah called out as she shut the car door.

Destiny was silent on the way home.

"Did you have a good day at school, darling?" Anne asked.

Destiny reeled off her day, however Anne sensed her mood and her granddaughter was quieter than usual. Being kept in the dark and wondering what the news was all day must have taken its toll. They were quiet for the rest of the trip. Anita was at the door when they arrived and gave Destiny a huge hug.

Destiny frowned but smiled at the same time.

"Tell me all about your day," she said, barely containing her excitement.

"Mmmm, it was all right," Destiny said warily but told Anita all that had happened.

"Jesus and Gershwin, oh wonderful!" she said. Turning to Anne, Anita said: "See, we picked the right school. They have a good academic reputation."

Anne nodded.

"Are you hungry? Here, let me get you a glass of milk and some shortbread biscuits."

"Yes, please!" Destiny smiled.

"Just a snack. You don't want to spoil your dinner. Tonight, we are having a simple spaghetti bolognese with some garlic bread. And for dessert, I bought you a nice apple turnover from the bakery. Just half. I want the other half! What do you think?"

Destiny beamed.

After dinner, Destiny fed her cat Sparkles and helped Anita and Anne wash the dishes.

"Go and watch some TV, Destiny. We'll be right with you," Anita said.

Destiny wheeled herself into the living room and settled into some evening shows. She could hear Anita and Anne whispering in the kitchen. *What's with all the mystery?* she wondered. Presently, they joined her. Anne switched off the television as Anita sat in the chair next to Destiny.

"We have something very important to tell you, Destiny," Anita said softly.

Anne smiled and sat next to Anita.

Anita let out a big breath.

"Ever since you came to live us, you have filled both our hearts with great joy. So, we are going to make you a proposition. You don't have to give us an answer straight away. We want you to think carefully about what we say and make your own decision."

"What's a proposition?" Destiny said seriously.

"We're going to make a deal with you. Just relax," Anne chimed in.

"Okay, here we go. We love you so much and never want you to be alone in this troubled world, so we have decided that we want to adopt you. It's a very big move for all of us. Now, don't be in a hurry to make up your mind. Take your time, talk to your friends if you want to," Anita said as she relaxed back into her chair.

"You will need to talk to the remaining members of your family. We understand. We can talk to them for you, if you wish."

Destiny had some aunts, uncles and cousins she hadn't seen in a long time. Her grandparents on both sides had since passed on. Her parents married later in life and had had just one child, Destiny.

Destiny was silent, at first. She stayed that way for a moment as Anita and Anne exchanged anxious looks.

Then it came, slowly. She felt the corner of her mouth twitch a little and she started to smile, just gently. Both women sighed.

"I don't know what to say," Destiny confessed.

"You don't have to say anything just yet, young lady," Anne said with a serious expression.

Anita let out a laugh as the three of them smiled at each other.

"What do I have to do?" Destiny said.

"Nothing but make the decision to be ours. We will look after everything else," Anita said.

"Do I get to keep my name?" she asked cautiously.

"Yes, of course, if that's what you want, darling girl," Anne said. "Adoption is a legal measure to protect you. It means we can plan our futures together. It's not about money, either. Anita's father made sure we were financially secure before he died. He would have been so proud of you." Anne caught her breath and reached for her handkerchief, dabbing her eye.

"You won't be cut off from the rest of your family, either. You will be able to visit them, and they you, as much as you want," Anita said.

"Mmm," Destiny said smiling. Then she yawned.

"You're tired. It's Saturday tomorrow. We need to do some shopping. You can help," Anita said, placing her hands on her lap. "Come on, tiger, let's get you settled."

Anita got up and put her hand on Anne's shoulder. Anne blew her nose, loudly, which made Destiny giggle.

Wheeling down the hallway to her bedroom, Destiny was soon in her pajamas and in bed.

"Sleep tight. Don't let the bed bugs bite," Anita said, turning off the light and closing the door. "Ooops," she said, opening the door again. "You have a visitor."

Sparkles the ginger cat came bounding into the room and leaped on Destiny's bed. Destiny lay in the darkness and looked out the window. A big, bright full moon shone its beams through to break up the dark room.

She dozed.

She saw her parents with her mind's eye. They were smiling at her. Then she heard the screeching of tyres and smashing glass. Tossing and turning with her upper body, a light sweat formed on her brow. She threw her head from side to side then opened her eyes.

Reaching for her phone, she put in her ear plugs and tuned in to her favourite radio station. She wasn't able to concentrate on the music and pulled out the ear plugs. Looking next to the bed, she laid eyes on her wheelchair. Leaning to drag it closer, she managed to pull herself on to it and wheeled herself around the room, bumping into the bedroom furniture.

Sparkles sensed her distress and jumped onto her lap. She sat there stroking him and then, looking out the window, she saw it – a shooting star. Her heart leaped and she said to herself: *"Buttondrop!"* She closed her eyes. Soon she was asleep.

SANTA ROSA

CHAPTER 3

THE DREAM BEGINS

Floating. Destiny felt the sensation of rising and saw herself in her wheelchair with Sparkles on her lap.

That's strange, I just went through the roof. Have I done this before?

She saw the halos of the street lights as she hovered over the city. Up, up she went into the open sky and saw the full moon and stars shining in the darkness. Mountains rose up and wide open plains with lakes and rivers. The piebald rocking horse appeared which made her feel wonderful. She remembered him from the first dream. She climbed on to its back and settled in for the ride. Together they flew over great cliffs out to the open sea. She didn't feel the least bit afraid. The rising sun appeared on the horizon as they moved over the great expanse of water. A dot in the distance slowly grew larger – a sailing ship with great sails unfurled and shining in the sun. Gently the piebald horse descended, down, down towards the ship and landed on the deck. No one was around. She stayed mounted and wondered what was happening. Then a cabin door opened and out he came – Buttondrop. Buttondrop the Maptoodoo.

"Oh!" Destiny cried and jumped off the rocking horse. She ran to his open arms.

"Dear child, we meet again," he said softly. She held on to him with both arms. He encircled her with his – a happy reunion. Her memories of the last adventure came flooding back.

He was the Wish-Master who protected her. He made dreams come true.

She danced, then realised something strange – she was walking. She once more felt the power in her legs as she ran around the deck.

"Slow down, child," Buttondrop laughed and he held his belly.

A young girl poked her head out of the door. Destiny stopped.

"Ah, Jessica, we have a visitor," Buttondrop said.

Others appeared – the crew. They were curious about this stranger.

"Come forward, don't be shy," Buttondrop invited.

Slowly the crew came out and gathered on the deck. The young girl Jessica approached Buttondrop and Destiny, with her hands held behind her back, did a little skip and joined them.

"Destiny, this is Jessica. She is one of my crew and will be looking after you while you are with us."

Jessica stepped forward and offered her hand but kept a straight face. Destiny smiled as they shook hands.

"Pleased to meet you, Jessica, my name is Destiny. I hope we will be great friends."

Jessica beamed.

"Scurvy rats, get back to work," a crusty old sailor shouted. "Stop gawking, back to it."

There was mumbling among the sailors as they went about their business.

"Set sail for Hilltopia," Buttondrop commanded.

"That's Hieronymus. Don't worry about him, his bark is worse than his bite," Jessica said taking Destiny aside.

"We were told a visitor was coming but Buttondrop didn't say who," she said. "I'm glad it's a girl. I am the only girl on the ship." Jessica laughed. "We're going to Hilltopia to pick up some more passengers. Welcome to life on the big seas."

"How exciting!" Destiny exclaimed.

"Come on, let's go below deck. Ooh, what are you wearing? You're still in your pajamas! Let's get some proper sailor's clothes for you," Jessica said.

Jessica took Destiny's hand and led her below.

"Buttondrop keeps all the clothes in his cabin. Now, what have we got? No, no, definitely not," Jessica said as she sorted through the outfits.

"How about this! A big bow!" Both girls giggled. There were flounces and fitted tunics, caps and hats, skirts, calf-length trousers, tops and T-shirts, all in a wild assortment of styles and colours.

Destiny tried on a few of the outfits before deciding on a striped blue and white T-shirt, calf-length trousers and a pair of soft leather moccasins. A black beret with a pom-pom topped it off.

Sea birds circled above the sailing ship as they headed for Hilltopia Harbour. The wind was fresh and the sails full. The orange sun lowered in the sky filling the sky with a pink hue. The sea was calm as they entered the harbour. Steering to the berth, they moored. A crowd of onlookers gathered to admire the newest ship in town. Buttondrop, Destiny and Jessica walked down the gangplank on to terra firma.

Pushing his way through the crowd, Jack, the young boy who had freed Destiny, Manky and Shonky from Maximum Mischief's dungeon, presented himself and bowed.

"Oh Jack, it's you," Destiny cried, running and throwing her arms around him.

"Destiny," Jack said.

"Jack, my lad, how are you?" Buttondrop said.

"Fine, sir. I have been working on the fishing trawlers. Have you heard about Shonky?"

"What?" Destiny said. "Tell me, tell me!"

"He survived the fall from the cliff, Destiny, and was washed out to sea. Some fishermen found him and he is home now. Only problem is, he has lost his memory and doesn't know who he is or anyone else. He is with Manky and Angelique. Maximum Mischief burnt down Angelique's house and they are staying at the church," Jack explained.

"Oh," Destiny said, trying to take in all the information.

"We're going to collect them. They will join us on our sea voyage. Ah, the open sea!" Buttondrop sighed.

The companions hailed a hansom cab, pulled by a stout horse with a clean carriage.

"Have you ever been in one of these before, Destiny?" Jack asked.

"No, how exciting," she said.

They hopped in and directed the driver to the church. The ride through the town was thrilling. When they arrived at the church, they found Angelique, Manky and Shonky manning a soup kitchen in the front grounds. Angelique wiped her hands on her apron as they approached.

She didn't smile but a small tear welled in her eye.

"Destiny! Jack! It's so good to see you again," Manky cried as he ran up to them. They hugged each other tightly.

Shonky stayed behind the table and continued to ladle soup to the parishioners. He watched the goings-on very closely. Destiny caught his eye. She seemed familiar to him but he didn't know why. Buttondrop had cautioned her to treat Shonky gently. His mind was still frail.

"Hello, Shonky," she said.

He smiled.

Father Primus greeted the guests and Buttondrop took him aside.

"Oh, dear child," Angelique said.

"Angelique," Destiny said, embracing her.

"I heard what Maximum Mischief did. Horrible man, so wicked."

"He will get his comeuppance, don't worry. My house will be rebuilt, but meanwhile, we are going on a wonderful adventure on Buttondrop's ship. How exciting!" Angelique declared.

Father Primus approached.

"Don't worry about a thing, Buttondrop has explained everything. Your animals are safe in our stables until you return and your home rebuilt. I have others here at the soup kitchen who can take over your duties. Have a wonderful time! I'm jealous. I wish I was coming with you but I will get my chance, another time."

Manky, Shonky and Angelique went to collect their things.

"We take just what we need," Angelique said to the twins.

Arriving back at the ship, the companions stored their things and introduced themselves to the crew. Jessica stuck to Destiny's side.

"I'm feeling a bit tired," Shonky said to Manky. "I think I might have a wee lie down for a while."

"OK," Manky said. "We sail for the open sea in the morning. Have a nice rest."

Jessica took Destiny, Jack, Manky and Angelique on a tour of the ship. They admired the figurehead at the front, a beautiful woman.

"The name of the ship is the *Santa Rosa*, a clipper, very fast. She is sturdy and has weathered many long voyages. This is the galley where all the meals are prepared and here is the captain's cabin. The crew sleeps below deck in hammocks. You all have bunks in the guest cabins. Shhh, let's not disturb your friend," she said.

The crew busied themselves stocking up on supplies and preparing for the journey.

Shonky slept and dreamed. Again, faces and voices he didn't recognise came into his mind and he felt afraid. He saw a great stone castle and a dungeon. He saw fast flowing water and gigantic rocks. Pictures floated in his mind's eye of crashing waves and the sensation of falling. And then, a smiling face looked straight at him.

Manky!

He woke up and leaped out of the bunk.

I know who I am.

Memories flooded back. His parents, his brother, Buttondrop.

Destiny!

He ran up the ladder to the deck and looked around. He kept going until he caught up with Manky and the rest.

"Manky!" he cried. "I remember, I remember!"

Manky ran up to him and gave him the biggest bear hug.

"Oh, that's fantastic!" he said.

Destiny and the others gathered around, laughing.

"You rascal," Jack grinned.

Night approached and the companions enjoyed a hearty meal of vegetable broth with chickpeas and sat on the deck looking at the stars. The double crescent moons, named Kisal and Meb, lit up the clear, night sky. It was perfect weather for sailing and the friends discussed the big adventure.

"Buttondrop is teaching me how to navigate the seas by the stars. It's hard but I think I am getting it," Jessica said.

Everyone retired early. Destiny lay in her bunk and went over the day's events. *I wonder what Mum and Grandma are dreaming of,* she thought.

The harbour was quiet, all activity had ceased. "Ten o'clock and all is well," the night watchman cried out.

"Hoist the mainsail!" Buttondrop commanded.

Seagulls hovered over the crew as they scurried to their tasks. Buttondrop took the helm. "Steady as she goes."

The sails unfurled and caught the light wind fully. Slowly but surely the *Santa Rosa* edged away from her mooring. Onlookers from the shore waved goodbye and the companions clung to the rails waving back. The slight breeze barely rippled the water. Gently she steered out of the harbour entrance into the open water, leeward.

"Smell the brine," Angelique said. "It fills your senses."

"What is the name of this sea, Angelique?" Destiny asked.

"Peagreen. Peagreen Sea. There are many islands and places to visit. Buttondrop told me we are headed for Hermanstock Island, where a garrison of soldiers and sailors is based. I've never been there before. Apparently, it is a lovely place."

There was a commotion. A group of sailors were gathered around a barometer, which showed a high reading in the atmosphere. They alerted the captain.

"We're in for a blow," said Hieronymus who was teaching Jessica everything he knew about sailing. He was a crusty old salt with a tattoo of an anchor on his left forearm.

Jessica joined the friends.

"Hieronymus says we should prepare for a storm," she said with concern.

The wind began to pick up and dark clouds gathered in the midday sky. The barrelman was called down from the crow's nest and a light rain began to fall. The crew busily tended to the sails, securing them fast.

"Poseidon is sending us a gift," Buttondrop smiled as he joined his friends.

"I have a story for Count Dabacus," Destiny said. "I looked up the Greek gods in the school library. Poseidon is the god of the sea."

"We will be meeting up with Count Dabacus...you can tell him yourself," Buttondrop said.

"It's best now that you go below deck. We may be in for a rough ride. Batten the hatches!" he ordered.

The sea whipped in a frenzy and buffeted the *Santa Rosa* like a cork. Lanterns in the cabins swayed and the companions kept quiet listening to the ferocious wind and rain which lashed the ship. Waves crashed and then an almighty CRACK. The sail at the front of the ship had broken.

A cry was heard: "Man overboard!"

The crew in their all-weather gear rushed to the starboard side. A lifebuoy was thrown. The sailor, Benedict, struggled to stay afloat in the vicious and thrashing sea but grabbed hold of the lifebuoy as lightning flashed and thunder roared. A sudden jerk of the vessel had caused him to lose balance as he fastened ropes on the rail of the ship, tossing him into the angry cauldron.

"He's gone under!" someone shouted.

"Hold on, matey," another yelled above the din. A second lifebuoy was thrown. Spluttering seawater as the storm raged around him, Benedict made one last mighty effort to reach the lifesaving device. Holding on for dear life, his crewmates drew him in to the ship. Hoisted aboard to his waiting comrades, he was wrapped in waterproof blankets and carried below deck for the ship's doctor to check.

"Close call," Buttondrop said.

The storm lasted for an hour or two then all was calm, with just light rain falling.

"We'll have to make our repairs at Hermanstock," Buttondrop said.

Limping into the harbour, they saw before them a lovely sight, the settlement called Penstown. It was set on the shores of a natural harbour and was a meeting point for many ocean-going travellers. A gentle breeze ushered the *Santa Rosa* into a crowded harbour and they moored. It was a fine day.

"We will stay here until repairs are done," Buttondrop said.

Destiny went up to him.

"What can we do, Buttondrop? We'd like to help."

Angelique, Manky, Shonky, Jack and Jessica gathered around.

"We need to get more supplies. All our stores and foodstuffs were ruined in the storm. Go into town and stock up. I've made out a list of what we need. Hieronymus will accompany you. How does that sound?" Buttondrop beamed.

They all clapped with glee and anticipation although tinged with a little sadness over the difficult situation they faced.

They set off.

"Wait for me," Hieronymus called out, trying to put his jacket on and comb his hair at the same time.

"Hurry up, old man," Jessica laughed.

Penstown was set at the foot of hills which stretched back into the heart of the island. The companions joked and laughed as they sauntered along the dirt road leading to the town. Hieronymus consulted his list.

"OK, first we should go to the store. Yes, yes. Oh, Buttondrop forgot one thing."

He pulled a pencil out from his jacket and wrote on the list.

Townsfolk mingled as the group entered the main street. Ladies in fine dresses and carrying pretty parasols were accompanied by their gentlemen. Storekeepers in white aprons tended to their display tables outside the stores. *Everyone seems so happy*, Destiny thought. Wooden shops lined the way as they found the general store and entered. Destiny feasted her eyes on the array of goods on offer.

"Jessica and Destiny, I need you to find a few things," Hieronymus said. "Fresh vegetables and fruit. Here, take a basket each for incidentals and a notebook and pen to write down what you have ordered to be delivered. Off you go. Meet us at the front counter.

"Manky and Shonky stay with me. Angelique, we need herbs and spices. Surprise us with what you find. Jack, here is a list of kitchen utensils the cook wants."

They all went their own ways.

First up, Hieronymus and the twins went to the butchery and ordered barrels of pickled meat. Sacks of flour, rice and dried beans were also on the list. Then they went to the drinks section and checked out the barrels of cranberry juice.

"Very important when you're at sea," Hieronymus said seriously.

Having purchased everything they required, the happy shopping troupe gathered at the front counter and chatted while Hieronymus settled the bill and organised for the supplies to be delivered to the *Santa Rosa*.

"Who's hungry, hmm? I think we should go to the tavern and have some lunch. They serve very good meals and I'm keen for a pint of beer!" Hieronymus said cheerfully. They made their way to the tavern, The Pig & Pen, and found an empty table. They looked around at the décor and the patrons excitedly. Manky and Shonky pored over the menu as Hieronymus went to the bar.

"A pint of your best, bartender."

Destiny's eyes wandered. They landed on a little boy at the table next to them. *Oh, you remind me of someone at school,* she said to herself. He was with a grown man in a soldier's uniform, a red tunic with epaulets. She caught his eye. He smiled. He jumped off his seat and came over and said to her in a loud, strong voice: "I've got something to tell you!"

Destiny was baffled but kept silent.

"Follow me water, all the way ups!" he shouted.

Destiny's jaw dropped.

"What did you say, little boy?" Shonky said with curiosity.

"Follow me water, all the way ups!" he repeated.

They all burst out into raucous laughter. The little boy seemed as proud as Punch.

"That's so funny!" Manky said. "But what does it mean?"

The boy shrugged and put out his open palms. The soldier approached.

"He heard it in a dream and now we can't stop him from saying it!" the man said with a twinkle in his eye.

"Pardon my manners, my name is Maximilian Bowers and this is my son, Tom," he said, offering his hand.

"My Dad's a sergeant," Tom said, chuffed.

"Can I get you a beer, my good man? Please, join us," Hieronymus offered.

The noise in the tavern was deafening with hollers and shouts. The Pig & Pen did a good trade and the publican was an affable man named Hans Haanstra. He was missing his right arm which was lost tragically in an industrial accident when he was younger. This only added to his fine bearing. He had good standing in the community and had a seat on the town council. He mixed and mingled with the patrons.

"Hello, Hans! How's life treating you?" someone shouted.

"Never been better!" he shouted back over the din. "Don't forget to get your tickets in the raffle, kind sir. There are many fine prizes to be won. How are you for drinks? Waitress!" he said cheerfully, his generous girth jiggling with merriment. He moved on to another table. The group ate heartily, Hieronymus finished his beer and they bade farewell to the soldier and his son. They hit the road.

Shonky sang:

Follow me water, all the way ups!
Follow me water, drink from the cup.
Tasty and sweet, cool on my tongue,
Too many cups and I'll come undone!

"Shaddap Shonky!" they all said, laughing. "It didn't take him long to get back to his old ways!" Manky said with amusement. Shonky lit up.

It was just coming on dusk as the companions arrived back at the harbour. Repairs on the *Santa Rosa* were completed. Penstown shipwrights were renowned for their quick and thorough work and there was a quick turnaround for damaged ships that made their way there. The supplies from the town had been delivered and everything was ship-shape. The crew huddled, cross-legged in small groups around the deck. Buttondrop approached Destiny with his hands behind his back.

"I got this for you. Would you do us the honour of playing something?" he said, producing a clarinet. Destiny's eyes lit up.

She started playing a soft, lilting tune and everyone went quiet. One of the sailors disappeared below deck and returned with his accordion. He nodded to Destiny and they started up a riotous jig which had the others on their feet in no time, dancing and laughing. Hieronymus grabbed Jessica by the waist and waltzed her to the beat.

The twin moons were in their crescent form and the stars twinkled in the sky. It was a fine night.

CHAPTER 5

THE ISLAND THAT HAS NO NAME

Destiny woke up early and dressed in the faint light. All the others were still fast asleep. She climbed the cabin stairs and went out on the deck to the front of the ship. Light was breaking on the horizon in lovely reds, yellows and pinks as she looked around. Soft bundles of clouds peppered the sky and the sea lolled gently in the fresh breeze.

"Good morning, child," she heard a soft voice behind her say. She didn't look around, she knew it was Buttondrop.

"Good morning. What a beautiful day! So calm."

The two stood in silence admiring the view. Waves gently lapped the *Santa Rosa* and they saw some flying fish leap out of the water. Sea birds dived on them.

"Where are we going, Buttondrop?" Destiny enquired.

"Ah, a very special place. I have a very special surprise for you. Be patient, we will arrive there this morning."

Destiny decided it was the right time and began to tell Buttondrop about her Mum and Gran and the adoption. He listened intently.

"I can't stop thinking about Mum and Dad and what they would think," she said.

Buttondrop smiled.

"A very big decision, one you will have to make on your own, young lady. Don't worry, you'll get all the help you'll need. Talk to your friends, they have a lot of wisdom to impart."

Shonky joined them, yawning and scratching his belly.

"Loved the music last night, Destiny, such fun! The others are still fast asleep. Should we wake them?" he asked.

"No, leave them, they will rise when they are ready," Buttondrop said.

The crew went about their daily business while Buttondrop consulted with the helmsman. Maps were studied and there was much discussion. A brisk breeze filled the sails and the *Santa Rosa* picked up speed. Destiny enjoyed the full wind in her face as she and Shonky leaned over the rails to watch the water splash. Manky, Jessica, Jack and Angelique soon joined them and they chattered excitedly about the big surprise.

Buttondrop gathered the friends and crew together.

"This is a secret place we are about to visit. A secret island of children. A refuge, if you like. I want you all to swear now that you will keep this a sacred secret. I know I can rely on you to do this. Take a moment to yourselves," he said.

The gathering fell quiet for a minute or two and then there were smiles. Everyone understood the importance of this place to Buttondrop and they would all keep their word.

"Land ahoy!" Hieronymus hollered.

There was no wharf to moor at, so they dropped anchor and launched the rowing boats to make their way ashore. Some of the crew were assigned to stay with the ship while a select few manned the oars.

They reached the shore and clambered out of the boats. The vegetation was thick with tall trees towering over wild underbrush and huge boulders. Cutting its way through this was a walking path to the interior of the island. A dazzling array of birdlife filled the cool air with their songs and although they couldn't see them, small animals darted on the ground making rustling noises.

A clearing appeared and they encountered a group of timber buildings with thatched roofs nestled at the foot of a small, grassy hill. No one seemed to be around. A portly old man with a grey beard came out of one of the buildings and threw his hands into the air when he saw Buttondrop.

"Old friend, I haven't laid eyes on you for I don't know how long! Welcome, welcome all."

Buttondrop introduced the man as The Good Citizen and told the group he was in charge of running the island. They took turns shaking his hand and offering their names.

"The children are just in morning lessons. We would be honoured if you would give the class a brief lesson, of your own choosing. I am just about to give a lesson myself.

Come with me and we shall sneak into the back of the class." He motioned for them to follow him.

Angelique, Manky, Shonky, Jack, Jessica, Destiny and Buttondrop entered the room without a fuss and found some empty chairs at the back. The Good Citizen went to the front of the class. He nodded to the teacher, a red-haired woman called Miss Fox, and addressed the assembly.

"Today we are going to learn the days of the week, in French."

He drew on the blackboard, *lundi*.

"Can anyone guess what day this is?" he asked, smiling.

The class was silent.

"Monday," he said.

Miss Fox went to the piano.

"OK, I am going to teach you a song that will help you learn the days of the week."

She started to sing:

Lundi matin, l'empereur, sa femme est le petit prince,
Sont venus chez moi pour me serrer la pince.
Mais comme j'etais parti,
Le petit prince a dit,
Puisque cette ainsi nous reviendrons mardi.

The children soon picked up the tune and sang along to the words written on the blackboard. *Lundi, mardi, mercredi, jeudi, vendredi, samedi, dimanche.*

The sound of song filled the air, competing with the birds themselves. The crew members who stayed outside sat around, amused. They had picked up bits and pieces of different languages on their travels and vaguely understood the words.

"Now, children, we have a very special guest for you. This is Buttondrop the Maptoodoo. He is very wise and learned and will give us a short talk. Pay attention now." The Good Citizen moved to the side as Buttondrop took the floor.

"Good morning, children," he said.

"Good morning, Buttondrop," they replied.

"Today I would like to talk about self-esteem. Can anyone tell me what I mean by self-esteem?"

A little girl put up her hand.

"Yes, young lady. Tell us your name first."

She stood up.

"My name is Louise. Self-esteem is feeling good about yourself."

"Excellent," Buttondrop said.

"And can anyone tell me how we build our self-esteem?"

Destiny at the back of the classroom shot up her hand.

"Oh, oh, I know this one, Buttondrop!"

The children laughed and turned around to look at her. Shonky chuckled but got a stern look from Angelique.

"I told this to my classmates back home. My grandmother taught me – find something you are good at and build on that."

The children whispered to each other.

"Which brings me to my last point, the nature of self, I or me," Buttondrop continued. "Self is the only adventure in my humble opinion. When I start with myself and feel good about myself, I have so much to give others. Setting an example is very important. So, relax, keep the good feeling and everything else will follow naturally. Any questions?"

None of the children had any questions but Buttondrop noticed a little boy snarling. He called Miss Fox aside.

"Why is that little boy snarling?"

"Watch that one," the teacher said.

"I want to have a talk to him after class, please," Buttondrop said.

The Good Citizen, Miss Fox, and the children all applauded.

"Now, time for lunch. We will enjoy a stroll in the forest after lunch. Cook has a very special treat for your dinner – a vegetarian feast! How does that sound! There will be rice pudding for dessert."

They all filed out of the classroom. Miss Fox detained the boy and told him to wait a moment.

"Hello, what's your name?" Buttondrop said.

"Patson," the boy answered sourly.

"OK, Patson, tell me, what do you like doing?"

"Fishing in my canoe," he said warily.

"Very good, I suggest you keep that up. Do you go out with your friends?"

"No, I like going out alone," he said.

The snarl started to disappear from his face.

"When I was a young man, I liked hiking up in the mountains. I always went alone. Ah, the air was so fresh and clear up there. I can still smell it. I would take a little food and water with me in my backpack. Make sure you do the same when you go out in your canoe," Buttondrop said.

The boy began to fidget.

"Off with you then," Buttondrop said and joined his friends. They said farewell to The Good Citizen and headed back to the boats.

"The fun's not over yet," Buttondrop said with a mysterious smile.

They reached the beach and watched puzzled as Buttondrop looked around for some coconut trees. Finding some empty coconut shells, he waded waist-deep into the water and began shaking and clapping the shells in the brine.

"What's he doing?" Manky said.

The friends watched carefully from the shore and then let out a cry when a pod of dolphins arrived and surrounded Buttondrop. They were golden in colour and must have numbered about 20. They frolicked around him, diving and splashing and waving their fins in the air while swimming on their backs

"Come on, they want to give you a ride!" Buttondrop shouted.

Jessica, Jack, Destiny, Manky and Shonky joined him. Angelique stayed behind with the rest of the crew and put her hands to her face in awe. The crew members just smiled. They'd seen Buttondrop do this before.

The golden dolphins swam around the group and gently nudged them. Some lay on their sides and just flapped their fins. It was a sight to behold. They each climbed on a dolphin, and as a group headed out to the reef. Looking down, they were dazzled by the variety of marine life – turtles, fish, sea horses, starfish, coral, octopuses, sea cucumbers, you name it, it was all on show. They bobbed and skimmed across the top of the water at great speed, the riders being careful not to fall off. Over and through the waves they went, laughing and pointing at each other as they had a fantastic time.

"Woohoo!" they cried, fists punching the air.

Across the swell they darted, not a care in the world, just relishing the sheer joy of the moment, something they would remember for the rest of their lives. White breakers indicated they were close to the reef.

"Shark!" Shonky shouted suddenly.

They saw the unmistakable sign of a dorsal fin breaking the surface. The pod slowed down. A few of the dolphins broke away from the group and headed for the intruder. A scary tension filled their hearts. The dolphins circled the shark but didn't engage. The companions weren't sure but it looked like a tiger shark, not one to be messed around with, that's for sure.

"What do we do?" Destiny cried.

"We wait," Jessica said.

"Sharks are normally very wary of dolphins. They'll sort it out."

"Shonky, stop splashing the water!" Jessica said crossly.

The shark was in no hurry to go anywhere. He swam slowly but wasn't able to approach the main pod, being pinned in by the few that had broken off. Some seagulls had arrived and began to dive-bomb the predator, causing the shark to thrash in the water. Baring his rows of sharp teeth, the shark lashed out at his attackers. One of the dolphins rammed him at great speed causing the predator to reel and retreat. He recovered and headed straight for the main group. The dolphins gave chase, butting the shark with their noses and trying to divert it from the stationary pod.

Then, with a flick of his tail and with no warning, the shark turned around and headed away.

"Whew! That was close," Manky said.

Jack laughed heartily.

"Love it!" he said. Not all the others shared his mirth.

Terrified, they headed back to the shore where Buttondrop, Angelique and the crew, who were waiting anxiously and had witnessed the fearsome attack. The group gasped for breath from their efforts to escape, as they recounted how close they had come to a sticky end.

"Goodness me!" Angelique declared, trying not to look concerned.

The crew had been fishing in the meantime and happily shared their catch with the golden dolphins, who swallowed the tasty fish in one gulp. They departed as the water gently lapped at the group's feet. The friends stood on the shore and waved goodbye.

I will never forget that, Destiny thought.

THE GREAT QUAY

The adventure continued unabated and all the friends were having a hoot. The sea voyage was agreeable to everyone and, wide-eyed and curious, they were lapping up the new experiences. Buttondrop, for his part, gently guided them along the way, checking on their welfare and safety and making sure they were having the time of their lives.

Destiny and Jessica were sitting on the deck chatting when all of a sudden the wind dropped and the sails went limp. They had entered the doldrums, or the calms as sailors sometimes called them, where sailing ships were left dead in the water due to no wind.

Hieronymus joined them and explained what was happening.

"Don't be too worried," he said reassuringly. "This is a common event out on the open sea. There is nothing we can do but wait till the wind picks up again. Here, I've got the line and tackle ready – let's fish!"

"Where are we headed, Hieronymus?" Destiny asked as she baited the hook.

"Ah, you'll see. Just be patient, something special. Whoa! I think I've got a bite," he shouted.

Manky, Shonky, Jack and Angelique joined them.

"What are we using for bait?" Jack asked.

"Small fish we caught by net," Hieronymus said as he wrestled with the rod, reeling in, letting go, reeling in. A splash in the water revealed quite a big fish. It struggled for a while but then went limp, defeated. Hieronymus reeled the catch up and it landed with a plop on the deck. He beamed a big smile.

"Cook will like this one," he said.

"This is a fish we have nicknamed poulet, chicken of the sea. It's yummy cooked just right," Jessica said, admiring the trophy.

One by one, the fishers reeled in their catches. There seemed to be plenty of fish waiting to be snared.

"We shall feast!" Buttondrop said as he joined them.

The cook came to look at the catch, wiping his hands on his white apron.

"I shall cook these very lightly in oil and we will have rice and vegetables," he said.

He gathered it all up in a cloth sheet and retired to the galley to prepare the meal.

"I'm starving, I can't wait!" Shonky said, rubbing his belly.

They all laughed.

Out of nowhere, the gang was drawn to eerie sounds coming from the ocean.

"That's whale song," Hieronymus explained. "Listen carefully, it is one of the most beautiful sounds you will ever hear out at sea."

In the distance, they saw a magnificent sight – giants of the sea leaping out of the water and crashing down with a mighty splash.

"That is called breaching," Hieronymus said. "These are humpback whales and they are migrating to warmer waters for the breeding season. Take a good look, they are putting on a special show just for us."

Everyone on board was transfixed by the spectacle. Slowly, the pod moved out of sight, continuing their journey.

"Land ahoy!" shouted the barrelman from the crow's nest.

Everyone rushed to the rails. In sight was an island with a huge, dark cloud over it. First, though, they had lunch to enjoy. Sitting cross-legged on the deck, they devoured the delicious fare, throwing their scraps to the hungry seagulls.

"Anchors aweigh!" came a shout.

"The Great Quay," Buttondrop said.

"There is a volcano on this island which we will visit. It is called Benaback. It is mostly dormant, hasn't erupted in a very long time but you will see something fantastic," he promised.

Clambering into the rowboats, they headed towards land and drew the boats onshore. The sea was calm and the trip short. Inland they trekked, admiring the vegetation and small waterways along the way. The walk took two hours to the base of the volcano and they followed a well-beaten path upwards.

"C'mon Shonky, catch up," Manky shouted.

"Look what I've got, a lizard. He doesn't seem scared of me holding him either," Shonky said, showing the group his new friend.

"There you go, fella, off into the bush," he said, releasing the small creature.

The path was steep but they helped each other up, stumbling over loose rocks and volcanic ash.

"Keep going, just a little bit further," Buttondrop said, taking up the rear.

The path was well defined – obviously many had been using it in the past, a popular place for local islanders to enjoy. Slowly but surely they ascended the mountain, taking time now and then for a welcome break from the slog and to have a sip of refreshing water while admiring the spectacular view. Staying well hydrated was essential in the humid heat. They reached the summit.

"Now careful around the rim and don't look too hard into the crater," Buttondrop warned.

Looking down, they could see smoke rising from the bottom. Every now and then there was a puff of smoke and they were showered by what seemed like small stones. The smell of sulphur was strong in the air, pungent and acrid.

Angelique looked down into the crater and was transfixed. She stood staring down when one of the companions was alerted.

"Careful, Angelique, you heard what Buttondrop said," Manky said concerned.

Angelique couldn't break the spell of the sight before her and she began to have a waking vision, making her frown. She started to feel giddy and suddenly slumped to the ground closing her eyes.

"Angelique!" Destiny cried.

"Hieronymus, help me," Buttondrop said.

Together they got her to her feet and Buttondrop told the group it was time to head back down. They all followed the path in silence.

On the *Santa Rosa*, Angelique was made comfortable in her cabin with instructions to rest. Buttondrop stayed with her a while and she told him what she had seen. He listened in silence with a frown. *Is this a portent of what is to come?* he thought. He stroked his chin. He cautioned her to tell no one else but that they should keep it their secret. She closed her eyes.

Choppy seas kept the crew busy as the passengers milled on the deck or in their cabins. Destiny wandered onto the deck and found Manky seated, leaning against the base of the main mast carving a piece of wood.

"Whatyadoin'?" she said.

Manky smiled but didn't look up, continuing with his task. Destiny sat beside him.

"Tell me about you and Shonky, Manky."

"You first," he said with a grin.

"Oh, I was just thinking about home and what my Mum and Grandma were doing," she sighed. She went on to tell him about the adoption and how that made her feel. He listened. She told him about her best friend Sarah and how she made her laugh, about Sparkles, her cat, school, her wheelchair, and just life in general.

"We – Shonky and I – ran away from home when were very young," he said seriously. "Our Dad used to beat us and Mum, she didn't care, so we scarpered."

"We wandered the towns and countryside for a while and that's when Buttondrop found us. He took us to the secret island of children and we got some good schooling. You must never tell anyone about the island, it is a well-kept secret. Buttondrop told us that the island was set up by the High Council of Zenoth, which Buttondrop works for, and caters to street urchins, runaways, neglected children and anyone else of a young age that needs shelter and protection from the harsh world. Shonky and I were among the lucky ones, we were able to get help. Many can't," he said sadly.

"Cross my heart and hope to die," Destiny said.

Manky sighed.

"We then hooked up with Angelique and we haven't looked back since."

The two sat quietly together enjoying each other's company.

"I wonder how her new house is coming along?" Manky said.

"It was a terrible thing what Maximum Mischief did, nasty, mean old man," Destiny said.

"Ah, finished. This is for you," Manky said handing her a beautifully carved dolphin made from driftwood found on the beach when they encountered the golden dolphins.

"Oh, thank you so much, Manky. It is wonderful." Destiny gave him a big hug. Jack joined them.

"And here's something from me," he said.

He produced from his pocket a piece of bleached coral shaped into a ring. It was polished and smooth and had the lustre of mother of pearl shell. Destiny held out her hand but withdrew it suddenly.

"I can't wear that, Jack," she said softly. "You should give it to someone special."

Blushing and desperate not to look up and show his deep embarrassment, he put the ring back in his pocket. Watching, Manky looked concerned but decided to let it go for the moment.

"Ah, we few. We happy few!" Buttondrop chimed in as he approached, breaking the spell on the trio of friends.

"Angelique is resting. She had a terrible waking vision which she told me about but I am sworn to secrecy. Don't worry, we are all safe. Safe as houses!"

The sun was low on the horizon as the clipper nipped its way through the waves. The crew lit lanterns to light up the deck. Stratus clouds peppered the approaching night sky, the two moons glowing like soft globes as they rose in the firmament.

"Tonight, I will teach you something about how to navigate a ship by the stars," Buttondrop promised. He braced himself, inhaled deeply the briny air, thumped his chest a few times and snorted in a way only Buttondrop knew how to. The friends laughed.

"Ha! Snort like a little piggy!" Shonky shouted, pointing.

Buttondrop sniffed.

"It's actually a sign of well-being, I'll have you know young man," he said, frowning.

"Ha!" Shonky said.

"Shonky, respect!" Manky chastised.

Hieronymus arrived carrying lengths of rope.

"Gather round, me hearties, time to learn something," he said jovially.

The group hesitated a moment then Jessica said: "I'm off, I already know what Hieronymus is going to teach."

Destiny, Jack, Manky and Shonky gathered around the rope man.

Angelique said softly: "I'm in," as she joined the rope lesson. She had been withdrawn and quiet ever since the episode at the volcano and everyone respected her privacy and left her alone. They sat cross-legged in a circle and each took a piece of rope as Hieronymus began.

"Rope. Hemp. Very versatile material. Lay the end across your left hand with the free end hanging down. Form a small loop in the line of your hand. Watch closely. Bring the free end up to the loop and pass it through the eye from the underside (the rabbit comes out of the hole).

"Wrap the line around the standing line and back down through the loop (around the tree and back down the hole).

"Tighten the knot by pulling on the free end while holding the standing line. As simple as that. The bow line – basic but very useful. Try it yourselves," Hieronymus said.

The students were busy trying out their newly gained knowledge, comparing with each other, making mistakes, and working it out for themselves. The night began to fall and Buttondrop prepared his lesson. The sailors readied the *Santa Rosa* for the evening. The sun sank on the horizon like a huge orange fireball and the sea was calm as the stars came out from their hiding places to light up the sky.

"Steady as she goes," Buttondrop said.

CHAPTER 7

MAXIMUM MISCHIEF SETS SAIL

Rankle, Maximum Mischief's club-footed servant, knocked nervously on Mischief's study door. *Will he hit me?* he thought worriedly.

"What!" Mischief shouted.

Rankle opened the door and entered.

"News just to hand, Master.

"Buttondrop," he sneered, "has set sail for Peagreen Sea and has taken the brats with him. That Destiny has returned – cheek." He waited.

Mischief swivelled his chair and faced the open windows. *Ah, Peagreen Sea. It has been many years since I sailed her*, he thought. *What is Buttondrop's game?* he pondered.

Rankle fidgeted.

Suddenly, Mischief leapt from his chair and burst into a foul tirade, throwing desktop ornaments crashing and launching into a terrifying rant. Rankle ducked for cover and cowered in the corner. Oops! There goes the Venetian figurine, the sad clown face. Whipping up a ruckus, Mischief slowly calmed down and approached Rankle in the corner.

"Prepare my ship. Get Clotilda. We sail."

Rankle bowed and backed out of the room, fawning. He went hurriedly to seek out Clotilda and found her in the kitchen. He told her Mischief's orders and they both set about organising the crew. Among the castle's servants were a number of experienced sailors who began the task of loading provisions and seagoing gear onto a horse and cart.

"No time to lose," Rankle ordered, "we must make ship by nightfall, and don't forget the carrier pigeons."

Clotilda, in the meantime, packed her potions and magic spell books and pondered the next adventure with her beloved master. She smiled as she conjured up all the mayhem she could create. *Buttondrop*, she thought, *I'll get you yet. And you, Destiny, I'll have you back in the dungeon.*

A light drizzle of rain fell as the convoy set off to the harbour. Maximum Mischief rode in front in a horse and buggy while the others followed. Rankle and Clotilda sat together on one of the carts and talked in hushed tones about their next move.

"Angelique is sure to be there with them, and Count Dabacus," Rankle sneered.

Clotilda scowled and adjusted her hooded cloak. "When I get my hands on that Destiny," she said, menacingly.

The journey took quite a few hours and by the time they arrived at the dock, night had begun to fall. Hurriedly the minions unloaded the carts and took the gear and provisions up the gangplank to the waiting ship. Hard-bitten sailors on the *Nemesis,* Mischief's flagship, helped with the task. The captain of the ship was a shady character called Smarmy Smirker. He held a whip which he used freely on the hapless crew, much to their displeasure. Mischief made himself comfortable in the main cabin and summoned Smarmy Smirker who told him when the tide was due to turn so they could set sail.

"The morning tide is our best bet to make good headway," Smirker said. Neither of them smiled – smiling was discouraged on the *Nemesis.*

"Get on with it," Mischief snarled.

The crew were quiet during the night, whispering to each other what they had learned about their mission. There was unease in the air as they prepared for the next morning's departure.

In another part of the ocean, Count Dabacus and his small sloop were skimming the waves, happily unaware of Maximum Mischief's movements.

"Count, she is in fine form today," the master of the sloop said as the *Glorious* skipped over the water. Count Dabacus was dressed in full seagoing attire, complete with cap, and he laughed heartily. The plan was to rendezvous with Buttondrop and the *Santa Rosa* at Hermanstock. Using his special magical powers, he was in contact by mental telepathy with Angelique and they kept each other informed of events.

Count Dabacus was an old soul, from the planet Sarasia, known for its cultivation of magic and astral travelling. He had met Destiny once before and was eager to see her again. They had discussed the Greek gods and the Count wanted to tell her about their Roman counterparts.

Skipping over the waves, a smile was plastered on every face. The crew consisted of men and women and they were all the companions of Count Dabacus. They came from all parts of the dreamworld and had enjoyed many adventures together. Count Dabacus looked very smart with his outfit, as were all the crew, practical for the purpose of sailing but also very fashionable.

"Ship ahoy!" cried one sailor.

Count Dabacus reached for his telescope.

"She sails with no flag."

"She is fast approaching. What do you want us to do?" someone asked, nervously.

"Full speed ahead," the Count ordered.

The Count's captain said to him, "I don't like the look of this. She is bearing down on us."

"Yes, we use all our evasive tactics. Keep the crew focused and relaxed," Count Dabacus said.

Meanwhile, on his ship, poised for the attack, Maximum Mischief peered through his spyglass at the easy-to-be-destroyed smaller ship ahead.

"Make contact, hoist the Hissing Hell. I'm curious about this one," he said.

The water was choppy and hungry, smelling a fight. A stiff breeze filled the sails as the *Nemesis* bore down on its quarry.

"Get cracking, you scurvy dogs!" Smarmy Smirker screamed above the winds as he lashed out at the nearest sailor with his whip. The sailor cringed in terror and got another lashing for his trouble.

"She's tacking," a sailor yelled.

"Stay with her," Mischief commanded.

"Gotcha!" Mischief bellowed with satisfaction.

The *Nemesis* pulled alongside the *Glorious.* The sailors, already prepared with weapons, blew trumpets, flashed swords and threw grappling hooks as Count Dabacus and his crew floundered under the sudden onslaught. Overwhelmed and outnumbered, the weight of the attack was too much for the hapless crew. Helpless, they surrendered quickly to save themselves from further harm. Rounded up and their hands bound with rope, they were taken aboard the pirate ship and dumped on the deck. Huddled together, they waited. Count Dabacus lowered his eyes, trying not to draw attention to himself. The others were quiet.

Maximum Mischief appeared, casually munching on an apple as if strolling through an orchard on a fine summer's morning without a care in the world.

"Well, what do we have here?" he said as he walked around the forlorn group.

Spotting the Count's downcast face, he said, "You, stand up." He lifted his cap and smiled a nasty smile.

"Count Dabacus. Well, well, well. What a coincidence meeting you here."

"Maximum Mischief – I should have known," the Count said.

"I'd like to stay and chat but I have better things to do," Mischief said.

"Brand them!" he ordered. Rankle smiled. Clotilda rubbed her hands together.

The motley crew of the *Nemesis* fetched braziers, filled them with kindling and wood, and set the fires burning. Branding irons were brought and placed in the fires. The crew of the *Glorious* watched in horror.

Smarmy Smirker pointed to the Count.

"You first!"

The *Glorious* men and women cried out, "No!"

Roughly separated from the others, Count Dabacus was stripped of his shirt.

"Kneel!" Smarmy Smirker shouted.

A large branding iron with the initials MM was taken from the brazier. A hush fell over the assembled sailors as a crewman aimed the red-hot iron at the Count's back. The Count bit down on a piece of wood that was shoved in his mouth. The *Glorious* crew held their faces in their hands.

NEMESIS
MAX MISCHIEF

MISCHIEF VISITS LITTLE HAVOC

The torturer advanced, aiming his branding iron at Count Dabacus's back, his eyes burning with malevolence, his mouth forming an evil grin. Cutting the air with the branding iron with one hand, he beckoned with the other, menacingly. Count Dabacus shivered and braced himself.

Suddenly, out of nowhere, a flock of seagulls swooped on the crewman making him drop the iron. They attacked the pirate crew sending them running, pecking at them with their beaks, and scratching them with their talons.

"Wave!" a sailor shouted.

A freak wave rose in the sea and hit the starboard side rocking the *Nemesis* violently, splintering timbers, the wind roaring anger in support for Dabacus. Maximum

Mischief, in his cabin, fell out of his chair and landed with a rude shock on the floor. The crew of the pirate ship scattered. Shaken, Mischief ran out to the deck and ordered the branding to stop.

"Put them all in the brig!" he yelled. "We set sail for Little Havoc. I will be in my cabin.

"Don't disturb me," he growled.

Below deck, Count Dabacus reassured his crew.

"What happened?" one asked.

"I called in a few friends," Dabacus said with a grin.

"Whew, that was close," another said.

"What happens now?"

"I will try to send a message to Buttondrop," the Count said gravely. The crew all knew he had special magical powers, mental telepathy being one. They bowed their heads.

"In the meantime, we sit tight and don't draw attention to ourselves. Hopefully, we can get out of this dire situation," the Count said kindly.

In another part of the ocean, Buttondrop was in his quarters when he received Count Dabacus's telepathic message. He frowned. Destiny knocked on his door.

"Come in," Buttondrop called out. He rallied and put on a jolly face.

"Ah, young lady, I'm glad you came."

"You wanted to see me," Destiny said as she inspected his cabin. She sensed that he was slightly troubled but decided not to say anything.

"We haven't had a chance to talk. I want you to tell me everything that has happened since we last met. I'm sure you've had many adventures. Tell me them all. Here, come and sit over here at my desk," Buttondrop said, smiling.

"Oh, a telescope! May I have a look through it?" she said excitedly. "And a compass! What's this?" she said, picking up a curious contraption.

"It's a sextant, used for navigation," Buttondrop explained. He knew she was evading the question but he waited until she was comfortable.

"Well, I have something to tell you," she said eventually.

"Back in the real world...no, wait, not the only real world but you know what I mean."

She hesitated.

"My foster mum Anita and my gran Anne want to adopt me. I think I've already told you."

Destiny put down the sextant and moved over to where Buttondrop was sitting. She climbed onto his lap and put her arms around his neck, snuggling into his shoulder. Buttondrop held her with loving tenderness.

"My girl, that would be wonderful," he said softly.

"They're not Mum and Dad. No one can replace them." She began to cry quietly.

"No, no one can replace your parents. I don't think Anita and Anne want to replace them. They love and care for you deeply and just want to look after you," Buttondrop said.

Destiny listened to the sound of the waves lapping against the hull of the ship through the cabin window.

"Yes, but..." she stammered.

"But?" Buttondrop prompted.

"Something is missing and I don't know what it is. I keep seeing a picture of a boy in my dreams. I don't know who he is or what he wants from me," she confessed.

"Is the boy Jack?" Buttondrop asked, interested.

"No, it's not Jack. Silly Jack. He made a ring and wanted me to wear it. How silly is that?" Destiny said casually.

Buttondrop kept a straight face and didn't show any emotion.

"You should be kinder to Jack – remember what he did for you," he said.

"Yes, I know. He's such a boy!"

"How is school?" Buttondrop continued, changing the subject.

"OK, I guess. My best friend Sarah made the netball championships and won for us, the school. I am still playing the clarinet. Thank you so much for your gift. The school has put in ramps and things which make it easier for me to get to classes in my wheelchair. Anita talked to the headmistress."

"This boy you see in your dreams – don't worry too much about it just now, it will all become clear to you soon," Buttondrop said as Destiny slowly crawled off his lap.

"I guess," she said with a hint of sadness. "I'll see you later. I'm off to join the others. The sailors promised we can play blind man's bluff with them." She stopped.

"Are you all right Buttondrop? You look worried," she said.

"It's nothing, just a little matter I have to work out," he said, turning to her.

"Go and play your game. I will be out later."

Little Havoc came into view as the *Nemesis* approached. Home to cutthroats, thieves and vagabonds, the pirate haven was full of unsavory characters who sailed the high seas preying on unsuspecting merchant ships. It was a natural harbour protected from the elements, and the navy, which had heard of the lawless settlement, had been unable to detect its exact location. Rumours circulated throughout the other Peagreen Sea settlements of this mysterious and forbidding place. Maximum Mischief, Smarmy Smirker and the pirates felt right at home here, and as they docked the sailors talked of the rum and fighting they would enjoy.

Rankle hustled and bustled preparing for Mischief's disembarkation. Clotilda knew she wouldn't be welcome with the departing company so she retired to her bunk.

Maximum Mischief sat at his desk and pondered. *Buttondrop will surely hear of the Count's capture,* he thought. He went to the cupboard and fetched his crystal ball. Gazing into it, he saw his arch-rival Buttondrop preparing a flotilla of ships. *He's going to try and save Count Dabacus,* he said to himself. *Ah, the nerve! Two can play that game.* Rankle knocked at the door.

"Send runners to Posey Pete, I wish to meet with her," Mischief ordered.

Posey Pete was the unofficial leader of Little Havoc. She was known for her cruelty and she was ruthless with her enemies, ruling the settlement with an iron fist. Rain began to fall as the party left the *Nemesis.*

"Posey Pete will be at the tavern, I am thinking," Rankle said to Mischief. "It seems that we must go to her."

A large crowd was gathered outside the tavern, looking menacing.

"Fight!" someone shouted.

An all-in, drunken brawl started. Maximum Mischief and his companions moved out of the way as Rankle sheltered his master with a wide, black umbrella from heavy rain that had begun to fall. Fists flew and groans of pain were heard as the throng battled it out.

Onlookers let out shouts of encouragement. Squelching in the mud and the blood, broken jaws were nursed and black eyes were dished out aplenty. A rider appeared mounted on a chestnut horse – Posey Pete.

"Come with me," she said to Mischief.

The drunken brawl in the rain continued as Mischief and his party entered the tavern.

"Take no notice of them," Pete said, gesturing to the melee outside as a drunken fighter crashed against the window nearly shattering it into pieces.

"Bartender, beers all around." Pete led them to a room at the back of the tavern and closed the door.

"Let's get down to business," Mischief said, leaning forward on the table and clasping his hands together. "I require your services."

"I have a prisoner who my enemy wants to take from me. No respect, these days. He is assembling a fleet of ships to attack me. I need to protect myself. Your pirate fleet is idle at the moment. Sail with me," he said.

The bartender brought the tankards of beer.

"What's in it for me?" Posey Pete said.

"Once the fleet is defeated, you will be able to sack Hermanstock. She will be left unguarded. There is a stash of gold bullion in the main garrison which is all yours – if you help me."

Pete sat back in her chair and inspected her nails.

"Well, what say you?" Mischief said, impatiently.

Pete leaned across the table and said, "Deal."

"Excellent," Mischief declared, getting up from the table.

"We assemble off the coast of Angarrad in three days' time. Everything is arranged. We'll put Buttondrop and his disgusting friends to flight. I can picture it now," he said, looking wistfully into thin air.

Outside, the brawl continued in the mud. The party moved deftly past the drunken throng and returned to their ship. Count Dabacus and his crew sat quietly in their cells. A clap of thunder brought a heavy fall of hail causing the drenched fighters to run for shelter. An eerie calm settled over Little Havoc.

THE FLEET'S ASSEMBLE

Buttondrop stood at the bow of the *Santa Rosa* and surveyed the surrounding seascape. His face was stern and yet composed as he contemplated his next move. He had learned from Dabacus that Maximum Mischief was up to something dastardly and he anticipated that their next encounter would be a desperate and dangerous fight. In the distant sky, dark forms gathered and moved toward the ship.

"What's he doing?" Destiny asked Angelique.

"He's summoning the seabirds to him," she said. Buttondrop stood with his arms outstretched, reciting a mantra in words the others did not recognise. The clear sky became full of a colourful and wonderful spectacle as his summoning continued to full strength. Soon, the ship was covered in many kinds of seabirds – seagulls and albatrosses, auks and petrels, frigate birds, shearwaters, sea eagles, you name it. Buttondrop smiled as some landed on his head and shoulders. Destiny laughed heartily.

"Jack, Manky, Shonky, Jessica, come look!" she shouted.

The others rushed out to behold a spectacular sight as sea flyers of every shape and form squawked and fussed on the deck and masts of the ship, feathers flying everywhere.

Angelique and Hieronymus joined them.

"They are talking," Angelique informed them.

"What are they saying?" Manky asked.

"I don't know. We'll have to wait for Buttondrop to tell us," Angelique said.

Jessica started collecting all the feathers that were strewn across the deck.

"I can make a fine pillow with these," she said, laughing.

The sailors went about their business but kept a close eye on proceedings. They had been talking among themselves and sensed something big was about to unfold. Exactly what they weren't sure of but they were on full alert.

"I've seen some things in my time," Hieronymus said, "but I've never seen anything like this before."

Flocks of birds came and went as Buttondrop stood on the bow. Some perched on the arms of the main mast, others hovered in the air above the ship, yet others were busy catching a school of flying fish that skimmed close to the *Santa Rosa.*

The midshipman helped tie hand-written notes to the legs of the birds. Soon, all the flyers had departed with their messages. Buttondrop was calling for aid and he expected many to answer with their boats. He was counting on the Crumpled Faced People to come with their war canoes, supply ships to come from Hilltopia, rowing ships from Ecus Ligneus and, of course, the navy fleet stationed at Hermanstock.

Hieronymus gathered the young companions together.

"Buttondrop has instructed me to tell you what is going on with all this activity," he said.

"Count Dabacus and his crew are being held captive by Maximum Mischief on his ship, the *Nemesis*. Mischief is assembling a fleet of pirate ships to confront Buttondrop and his allies. How does Buttondrop know this? He has many spies, both human and animal, in his employ and his magic powers have warned him of Mischief's plans. You will all be safe as long as you do as you are instructed. This is a dangerous time for all of us but we are forced into a defensive position which we must exercise to the best of our ability. Buttondrop is so sorry that it has come to this, however events are out of his control."

The group was silent, absorbing all this terrible news.

"Our strength is in our action. We can overcome this grave situation if we stick together and watch each other's back. Choose a buddy to team up with and keep each other informed about what you are doing." Hieronymous smiled gently to reassure the scared companions.

"We are taking some rowing boats to Angarrad to collect coconuts," he said.

Angarrad was an ancient settlement of peace-loving people with a thriving community that harvested the fruits of the land and sea for sustenance. Many old buildings survived from their bygone heyday but served as sufficient shelter for the current inhabitants.

"Why coconuts?" Jack enquired.

"The ship's surgeon has requested we stock up on a ready supply of coconut water for the coming battle. Coconut water is very important in treating the wounded, it acts as an effective hydrator," Heironymus said gravely.

A delegation of townspeople awaited Buttondrop and friends at Angarrad.

"We have set up a makeshift hospital in the town reserve. We need to liaise with you about your requirements," a spokeswoman said. Throughout its history, Angarrad had acted as a refuge for the disadvantaged and wounded and had witnessed many great battles. The spokeswoman was a seasoned veteran of the conflicts that occasionally flared up in this part of the world. She had a vast medical knowledge of treating the wounded and infirm and was an expert in the administration of healing.

"Angelique, would you be able to look after this?" Buttondrop said.

"My pleasure," Angelique smiled as the townspeople gathered around her and led her to the reserve.

"We're off to collect coconuts," Hieronymus said, clapping his hands together.

"Who's coming with me?"

The party split up and went about their chores.

"We rendezvous here at sundown," was Buttondrop's final command.

"There is a special event tonight that I don't want anyone to miss," he added mysteriously.

The *Santa Rosa* lay moored in Angarrad harbour. Coral reefs stretched along the coastline and it was a very tricky exercise to navigate the breaks in the maze of reefs. The seagoing skills of the crew were tested to the limit. The afternoon soon came to a close, and as Destiny, Jack, Manky, Shonky, Jessica, Hieronymus and Angelique made their way back to the anchored ship, they gossiped excitedly about the special event.

The first order of business, though, was dinner. The ship's cook dished up a simple meal of fish and rice which everyone ate with gusto. He had prepared some of his famous sweet potato relish which never failed to please the hungry hordes. Fresh vegetables, which had been sought from the settlement stores, complemented the delicious fare. It was washed down with tasty ginger beer which put a smile on every face. Everyone gathered on the deck afterward.

"Tonight, we will witness one of the wonders of the natural world – a coral spawning," Buttondrop explained. He went on to tell them that once a year, not long after a full moon in early summer, the reef would erupt in a frenzy of activity as the coral released new life.

"We have snorkelling equipment for you all. Also, we have luminous filaments in a glowing solution in handheld, watertight containers which we will use to light the way in the water. Now, choose your snorkelling buddy, make sure to check on each other while you are out in the sea – and have the time of your lives," Buttondrop encouraged.

"Now, we wait," he said, leaning against the ship's rail. *All the indicators are right,* he thought. *Late spring, early summer. A few days after a full moon. She is so unpredictable about this, Mother Nature. Such a small window of opportunity for such a wonderful event.*

He smiled. He had not witnessed many of these special occasions but was always filled with wonder at the spectacular show put on by these mysterious sea animals.

The night sky was clear and the stars shone brightly. The excited group spoke in hushed tones, talking about what they would experience. Buttondrop had told them that the whole show only lasted from half to a full hour, so they had to act quickly to catch the phenomenon.

"It begins," Buttondrop said softly.

"Quickly now, go into the water and remember to check on each other," he said.

Water lapped gently against the hull of the *Santa Rosa* as the divers slipped into the murky darkness of the reef. Unfolding before their eyes was a spectacular show of millions of points of light rising up through the water to the surface. Schools of fish feasted on the eggs and sperm released by the coral polyps. The spores filled the divers' vision in all directions.

Occasionally, a swimmer would rise to the surface for air but soon plunged back into the action. They didn't have to descend too deep to enjoy the show and propelled themselves through the water with their flippers. The divers stuck together and as soon as the show had started, it was over.

Back on board the ship, the group was quiet at first then a raucous sound filled the night air as they compared notes of what they had just seen. Shouting with glee, their excited voices echoed across the water.

"It was like being inside a giant snow dome," Destiny said.

"Did you see the fish go ballistic," Jack chimed in, grinning.

"What's that smell?" Manky said. An unfamiliar and peculiar odour rose from the sea, making the group screw their noses up. They had never smelled anything like it and were at pains to describe the experience. All they could do was laugh at each other's funny reactions.

"That's the slick of the egg and sperm release. It doesn't smell too bad, does it?" Hieronymus said.

"Oh, and the colours!" Angelique exclaimed. "Stunning, beautiful!"

"I've never seen anything like it," Jessica said.

"Awesome! It was a snowstorm!" Shonky cried out, which made everyone laugh.

Talk turned to the coming battle as they packed away their diving gear in the ship's hold. None of them had been in a battle before and they were scared.

"We'll ask Buttondrop," Jack said. "He'll know what to do."

Destiny noticed that Jessica was shivering and went to her, giving her a loving, warm hug.

"Destiny, I'm afraid. I've never been in a battle before," Jessica said.

Together, they clambered back on the main deck, finding Buttondrop alone and looking into the night sky. They told him of their fears.

"I have arranged for all of you to be sheltered at Angarrad for the duration of the battle if that is what you want," Buttondrop said.

"This is a serious business and your proper safety is my main priority. No one thinks any less of those who choose to stay out of the coming battle. It makes perfect sense to protect yourself.

"Manky and Shonky have already told me they want to stay onboard the *Santa Rosa.* Jack, it is up to you whether you would like to join them." Buttondrop looked kindly at him awaiting his response.

Jack, head down, considered his options. He shot Destiny a quick look. He struggled to control the butterflies in his belly.

"I would like to stay with Manky and Shonky," he said.

Destiny spoke up.

"I would like to stay aboard too."

"Me too," Jessica said.

"Well, that's settled, I'm in. You two, I won't be letting you out of my sight," Angelique said to the girls.

Buttondrop closed his eyes in resignation. They had made their choice.

"It is settled then. All the arrangements have been made. As for Maximum Mischief, the real trick in fighting a battle is to get the enemy to defeat himself. We'll see what he is made of," Buttondrop said grimly.

Buttondrop left the group quietly and retired to his quarters. He pondered. Angelique had told him of her waking vision at the volcano, a great conflagration. He pressed her for the outcome of the disaster but she was unable to tell him. The safety of his people was foremost in his mind. A fitful, light sleep descended on his furrowed and sweated brow. Visions of fighting figures filled his mind's eye. He tossed and turned. Eventually, the disturbance subsided and he drifted off to a deep slumber.

AN ILL OMEN

Mischief was agitated.

Posey Pete and the pirate fleet were late for the rendezvous, his spies told him that Buttondrop had assembled a mighty fleet and the thought of Count Dabacus, that snivelling burden, was making him nervous.. *I need a plan of action,* he thought. A ruckus outside drew his attention.

"You scurvy dog, wait until Maximum Mischief hears of this," an angry voice said.

"No!"

Smarmy Smirker, the captain of the *Nemesis,* dragged a figure by the coat collar along the deck towards Mischief's quarters.

"What's going on?" Mischief demanded.

"Rankle!" he said, surprised.

"We have a traitor. Giving aid and comfort to the enemy. A whipping offence," Smirker said.

"Evidence," Mischief said. He was given hand-written notes. "And he has been smuggling food and medicine to Count Dabacus and his crew," Smirker sneered.

The crew was transfixed. You could cut the tension in the air with a knife. Everyone was silent.

"Bring me my whip," Mischief said, frowning.

"No! Mercy! I only did it for you, Master, see! Why should the Master make an enemy when he can make a friend? See!" Rankle pleaded. He was on his knees with his hands clasped, begging.

Mischief raised his whip in the air but then hesitated. Seeing his old faithful servant in such a sorry state sent waves of revulsion through his being. *What were you possibly thinking to betray me so*, he thought. Throwing his whip to one side, he stood still for a moment. Everyone watching froze in their footsteps.

"Enough," he said.

Smirker wiped his mouth with the back of his hand and stormed off. The crew returned to their duties.

"Come with me, old friend, we need to talk. You too, Clotilda," Mischief invited.

Clotilda smiled at being included in the inner circle.

"I want you to read the auguries, Clotilda. A mighty battle looms. I need some indication of how things will pan out. War is so unpredictable with many possible outcomes. I need just a glimpse."

"I will make preparations," Clotilda said taking her leave.

"You are weary from many troubles, Master," Rankle said, fawningly. For his troubles, he received a clip across the ear which lit up his face.

"Rest now."

Mischief went to his bunk and closed his eyes. His brow was fevered.

Clotilda pondered her situation. *Animal divination, yes, that will do nicely,* she thought. The ancient practice of animal divination was frowned upon mostly these days. It involved killing a beast and reading their entrails as a way of foretelling the future. It was a nasty business and not many practised it anymore: selecting a victim, slaughtering it and opening up its innards. Cold-hearted Clotilda was not shy of carrying out this grisly task.

Her attention was drawn towards the sky. The sun shone high and stratus clouds were strewn across the open blue. She imagined she was a bird, with a bird's eye view looking down on the sea. She pictured the ship and landed on it.

"Gotcha!" she said aloud as an unwary albatross cruised in for a landing. She pounced on the hapless creature and tied it with rope.

Some of the sailors approached.

"What are you going to do with that?" one asked Clotilda. She was silent.

"You know, it's bad luck to mess around with one of them," another said, referring to the albatross. This seagoing bird, quite large and majestic with a mighty wingspan wider than any other bird, was a favourite with sailors and many sea legends revolved around them. They had the tolerance to drink seawater and squid was said to be their preferred ocean catch. More sailors gathered around.

"It's my business," Clotilda said defensively.

Murmurs turned into shouts as the sailors showed their anger. Clotilda started to fear for her safety. One sailor tried to wrestle the captive bird from her clutches. She held on tight to her prey with one hand, fending off the would-be thief with the other.

"What's all the kerfuffle?" Smarmy Smirker intervened. The sailors were quiet.

"I've caught a pet and these men don't like it," Clotilda said. "They want it for themselves."

"Back to work!" Smirker said. The gathering tarried for a while but reluctantly dispersed slowly. Smirker knew these crusty old seamen and understood their concerns but was powerless to do anything. Clotilda was doing the bidding of Maximum Mischief who did not tolerate disobedience very well.

Clotilda picked up her prize and retired to her bunker. Word spread quickly among the crew about what the witch was doing. They suspected Maximum Mischief had ordered her to read the auguries about the coming battle and were horrified that she had chosen an albatross to kill and read entrails. The pirates were highly superstitious and killing an albatross was a bad omen. That night as they sat in small groups around the deck of the ship, they shook their heads and said to each other, "We're doomed." A dark cloud descended on them as they discussed the coming sea battle. Smarmy Smirker had briefed them on events and they had been busy organising weapons, rope and other tools of war, sharpening blades and cleaning rifles and pistols.

After committing the foul deed of killing the bird with feathers flying and opening the poor creature with sharp knives, Clotilda used her training to read the dead animal's entrails. She began to worry as she dissected the bird's innards, looking for clues to the future. The signs were not good.

I can't tell Master this, she said to herself.

She disposed of the carcass, cleaned up, and grabbed her lamp. She struck an eerie figure as she made her way to Maximum Mischief's cabin.

Not much was really known about Clotilda and how she ended up being with Mischief and Rankle. She had told Rankle that she was abandoned as a child and had been raised by three aunties who were considered witches by people in the village where she grew up. Their house was on the outskirts of the village and not many of the locals ventured close to their neck of the woods. As a young girl, she was trained in the dark arts and soon became very adept at casting spells and brewing magic potions. Her reputation was that of a ruthless and cold adversary and many avoided any contact with her. For her part, she revelled and delighted in this reputation.

"Well, what have you got for me?" Mischief looked at her menacingly.

As cool as a cucumber, Clotilda told him she had read the auguries and that the omens were favourable. A great victory was his to take. He looked at her with a penetrating stare.

"Good," he said, relaxing his grip.

The night hours passed slowly. An all-pervading uneasiness filled the air, and whispers in the darkness among the crew foreshadowed a terrible event about to take place. Many of the pirates were seasoned fighters, having terrorised the high seas for years. However, something told them this situation was different and unseen forces were at work against them. Being a superstitious lot, they desperately sought reassurance from each other that they would prevail in the coming battle.

Dawn broke and a huge red fireball poked its face over the horizon. The sea was generally calm although a bank of dark clouds lingered menacingly in the distance.

"They're here," a voice cried out.

Mischief fetched his spyglass. A great flotilla appeared on the horizon – Posey Pete had kept her promise. They anchored.

"Prepare for boarders!"

Rowing boats converged on the *Nemesis*, carrying the commanders of all the ships that had just arrived. There would be a pow-wow to discuss coming events. Maximum Mischief took the lead.

"You have all come. Ratchett, Boniface, and yes, even old Borogard! Ha! Welcome to my nightmare! Our common enemy, Buttondrop, awaits us. Great riches are in store for us if we win this battle. We will sack Hermanstock."

Mischief continued his speech. His audience was a collection of hard-bitten, crusty old pirates who knew a good stoush when they found one and this was one. For many years now, they had plied the great seas, plundering and wreaking as much havoc as they could on the law-abiding settlements of Peagreen Sea. This was the *coup de grace* for which many of them had been waiting.

"Fellow reprobates and assorted vagabonds, lend me your ears. The temptation of this gathering of salty seadogs is to settle old scores and get even with your adversaries. I say put aside these old rivalries, for together we face a greater foe that has ever assembled to challenge us. A greater prize that has ever put itself in our sights is within reach. I say we grab the opportunity with both hands and claim it for ourselves. Fight with me today, our time has come."

There was a hush among the gathering at first. Slowly smiles appeared and much handshaking and backslapping ensued. The taste of battle had filled their mouths and Mischief knew they would see it through to the bitter end.

The quiet morning and calm of the water belied the raging storm about to happen. The fateful day had begun.

CHAPTER 11

THE GREAT SEA BATTLE

A heavy fog, thick and wet, descended as the morning light unfurled. Both fleets were now fully assembled off the coast of Angarrad. The scene was set, the pieces were about to make their move.

Buttondrop signalled to his friends to wait. He made this communication by using flags that were hoisted high above the *Santa Rosa.* He ordered the Hilltopian supply ships to stay well behind the front line. The Crumpled Faced warriors milled around in their war canoes. The rowing ships from Ecus Ligneus sat patiently and the masters and commanders of the ships from Hermanstock busied themselves preparing for the fight.

Maximum Mischief kept in touch with his pirate fleet by means of carrier pigeons bearing written instructions. They flounced their feathers in anticipation and cooed heartily. They had been trained for this very purpose, to keep contact between seagoing vessels, and had a long association with sailors over the years.

The fog lifted.

Buttondrop took Shonky aside and whispered in his ear. The boy nodded and went to the front of the ship and climbed up on the bow. In a high, clear voice, he sang:

The minstrel boy, to the war has gone,
In the ranks of death you'll find him;
His father's sword he hath girded on,
And his wild harp slung behind him;
"Land of Song!" said the warrior bard,
"Though all the world betrays thee,
One sword, at least, thy rights shall guard,
One faithful harp shall praise thee!"

The Minstrel fell! But the foeman's chain
Could not bring that proud soul under;
The harp he loved ne'er spoke again,
For he tore its chords asunder;
And said "No chains shall sully thee,
Thou soul of love and bravery!
Thy songs were made for the pure and free
They shall never sound in slavery!"

Tears formed in some eyes and hearts filled with pride as the boy sang. Some who knew the battle hymn sang along softly under their breath. There was silence. Then from a place deep within, the sailors of Buttondrop's fleet let out a mighty roar of approval.

The order was given and one of the war canoes of the Crumpled Faced People paddled toward Mischief's fleet, teasing and tempting the enemy.

In a flurry of pigeon messages, Maximum Mischief told the pirate fleet to hold the line. Posey Pete couldn't wait any longer, she was itching for a fight. She broke rank and gave chase to the war canoe. The battle started.

One of the rowing ships targeted a vessel and rammed it directly midship. The hapless sailors leaped overboard as the ship quickly sank. Archers from the war canoes of the Crumpled Face People showered another ship with arrows, sending the pirates scurrying. A fire broke out on one of the ships sending the enemy panic-stricken into the choppy seas. All mayhem was let loose.

Destiny, Jessica and Angelique helped out with the wounded. The ship's surgeons were flat strap tending to the fallen. Manky, Shonky and Jack stuck close to Buttondrop.

The Hermanstock vessels were the next to engage the enemy. These were disciplined and experienced navigators with plenty of stories about their encounters with pirates. They hit hard at the centre of the pirate flotilla causing it to break up its defensive formation. Ships, in their confusion, scattered in all directions. Some rallied and struck back with a deadly force. The Hermanstock vessels reeled from the onslaught. Smoke and the roar of cannon filled the air.

The *Nemesis* drew up alongside the *Santa Rosa,* letting loose a volley of cannon shot that splintered wood and injured and killed many. Jack, Manky and Shonky joined the other companions in helping the wounded to assistance. Hieronymus guarded them as they helped with bandages and slings.

Pirates from the *Nemesis* threw grappling hooks at Buttondrop's flagship and swung with ropes onto the deck. The *Santa Rosa* crew rallied.

"Repel all boarders!" Buttondrop shouted above the din of the battle.

Hieronymus shepherded the friends to the surgery quarters. Once they were safe, he returned to the fray. Wielding his cutlass with precision, he put paid to many challengers. Still they kept coming, attacking relentlessly. Hieronymus fought off wave upon wave of pirates as they gained a foothold on the *Santa Rosa* deck. He was surrounded.

"Bring it on, you cowards!" he shouted at them defiantly.

He fought valiantly but was overwhelmed – there were just too many of them. One pirate swiped the back of Hieronymus's legs with his sword, crippling him. He fell to his knees, screaming in agony. He ripped his shirt and tried to wrap the bandages around his wounds to stanch the flow of blood. Still, he lashed out with his sword. He wasn't going down without a fight. It took five of them to subdue him. His stubborn resistance was not enough to save him though as his assassins closed in for the kill.

"I'm done for!" he cried before the final stroke was delivered. He fell.

Some fellow sailors took him to the infirmary.

"No!" Jessica cried. "Help him, doctor."

The doctor shook her head.

"I'm afraid this one's gone, young lady. I'm sorry," she said.

Jessica threw herself across Hieronymus's broken body, holding him tightly and sobbing. The others tried to comfort her. Some of the other young women sailors, who had been in the thick of battle, bowed their heads at the sight of their fallen mentor. Emboldened, they rushed back into the action with a ferocity that stunned the pirates who staggered back in terror.

Destiny held Jessica in her arms. Outside the battle raged.

Maximum Mischief began to panic, hitting out with his whip and sending servants scurrying. Things were not going his way.

"The line has broken!" a pirate yelled.

The pirate fleet began to disperse. Mischief ordered the *Nemesis* to withdraw.

"Set the prisoners free," Mischief commanded.

Smarmy Smirker gathered Count Dabacus and his crew on deck, lowered one of the life rafts into the water, and roughly shoved them all in, spitting and cursing at them as they clambered into the waiting boat. One of the crew fell, fracturing his arm. Dabacus hurriedly made a makeshift sling for the injured fellow.

"We had better not meet again," he said threateningly to Count Dabacus, waving a knife in his face. Dabacus just nodded his head but stayed silent. He didn't want to risk anything going wrong as they huddled in the raft. Pushed off with poles, Dabacus and crew paddled toward the *Santa Rosa,* slowly and surely through the now rough sea. Making rendezvous, they were helped aboard.

Safely on board the *Santa Rosa,* Dabacus was embraced eagerly by Buttondrop. They both laughed for a moment, a kind of scared, relieved laugh, but the weight of the moment soon brought serious looks to their faces.

The pirate fleet broke up and limped away in defeat, some taking refuge in Angarrad where hospital assistance for the wounded could be found. Efforts were made to collect those who had fallen into the water.

"We should pursue Mischief now and take him prisoner," one aide said to Buttondrop.

Buttondrop lowered his head quietly. The temptation was to deliver a swift and final blow to Mischief who floundered in the water, helpless. A few of Buttondrop's offsiders urged him to put the business to bed once and for all and ensure Mischief never tried this trick again. They protested loudly, making forceful arguments for further action.

Buttondrop, for his part, always relished the fight with Mischief and would never back down. Inwardly, he toyed with the idea of delivering Mischief a fatal blow. He struggled with this notion silently for a moment but then spoke up.

"No," he said, "he is broken. We allow him a little dignity. I know he wouldn't give us the same courtesy but we are not like him. We have to remind ourselves who we are, what we hold dear and what we stand for."

The Allies took stock of their casualties. The wounded and dead were tended to and makeshift repairs were made to the vessels that needed them the most. Fires were doused and the remaining ships gathered together for comfort and support. The Hilltopian supply ships came forward to lend a hand. Flotsam and jetsam littered the sea where the battle had just taken place. The smell of a great battle hung heavy in the air.

A mighty victory had been won. The hard-fought battle between titanic forces had set the sea alight with fire, smoke and the terrible sound of war. Remnants of Maximum Mischief's pirate flotilla were rounded up by the victorious forces of Buttondrop and secured.

Recovery was foremost in everyone's mind, celebrations would have to wait. It was agreed to take shelter in the harbour at Angarrad where facilities to help the fallen were located.

The Crumpled Faced warriors were the first to leave. They embraced their comrades in arms, smiled fondly, and spoke of all the stories they would have to tell once they returned home. Singing in unison with the women archers tapping their bows, they rowed out of view bound for their homeland.

The rowing boats of Ecus Ligneus hoisted banners high in the ocean air and raised their arms in tribute to their fellow victors. They engaged their oars and set off home too.

The naval ships from Hermanstock stayed behind to supervise the recovery as did the *Santa Rosa.*

Jessica was inconsolable. She didn't leave Hieronymus's side. Destiny and Angelique stayed with her. A sailor who had been with him at the last tried to comfort Jessica with details of his death and how bravely he faced his doom.

"He let them have it all, he didn't hold anything back. Hieronymus fought with a passion and fury I have seen in few men. He is a hero to many and saved many lives," he said.

"Doctors, you need to rest. The nursing staff have it now, we can manage the wounded from here," a nurse said. The ship's surgeons, men and women with blood-stained aprons, nodded and retired to their cabins.

"Count Dabacus, it is so good to see you! We heard what happened to you. Terrible," Destiny said. The Count and Angelique mingled with the nurses and wounded, offering help where they could. The calm after a powerful storm descended. It was time to heal.

CHAPTER 12

BURIAL AT SEA

Buttondrop gathered the companions together.

"Are we all here? Destiny, Jessica, Angelique, Manky and Shonky, good...Jack, my boy. We have been through a great ordeal but we are safe, although our work is not finished."

Buttondrop explained what would now happen with the dead and wounded. He also said the remaining fleet would clean up the sea of detritus left from the battle. He assigned the job of preparing the dead for burial at sea to the young group.

"I've never been in contact with a dead person before," Destiny said quietly.

"Just think of them sleeping," Buttondrop said kindly. "Stay close to Jessica, she is deeply distressed."

The bodies of the fallen seamen and women were laid out on benches in the infirmary, some on stretchers on the floor. The nurses showed the companions how to wash the bodies and prepare them for burial.

"There are so many," Jessica said, sadly.

The male and female nurses prepared canvas bags in which the bodies were placed and stiched shut with a special large sewing needle .

"He's ready," Jessica said.

The companions gathered around the body of Hieronymus and watched silently as the final preparations for the burial were completed. The bodies were taken to the main deck and laid out in rows. Sailors, dressed in full regalia, formed rank. Ceremonial flags were raised. Buttondrop, in his role as admiral, conducted the ritual. He spoke of the bravery of the fallen and how their efforts and sacrifice had secured a lasting peace for many years to come.

"Peagreen Sea is once again safe for merchants and travellers, thanks to you.

"We commit these sailors to the deep. May the spirits of the ocean welcome you into their open arms and protect you always."

Buttondrop gave a gold coin to the burial supervisor, as was the seagoing tradition.

Destiny stepped forward with her clarinet. She chose "Amazing Grace" to play. The lilting tones of the woodwind instrument summed up the sadness of the moment, and Destiny teased and coaxed the notes for maximum effect, letting the sweet sound envelop the gathering. It was a warm, sunny day and the sea was calm as the dead were farewelled. The sweet sounds of the clarinet lent much gravity to an already sombre occasion. Everyone was relaxed and tears were shed.

Hieronymus was the last to be committed to the sea. Buttondrop's personal arms flag was draped over him. Jessica stood close as the body gently slipped into the ocean. She smiled a little smile.

"Happy hunting," she said.

"They're in Davy Jones' Locker now," Manky said.

Count Dabacus and his crew broke into song, singing an old sea shanty. Their lovely voices lifted to the open sky filling the air with heartfelt sounds. Angelique led the assembly in a short prayer, asking the deities for strength and courage.

"We will take this time to rest and refresh," Buttondrop said. "I am so very proud of you all."

Destiny and Jessica joined a small group of young women sailors, sitting cross-legged on the deck. They spoke of Hieronymus and all that he had done for them as a teacher.

"My experience of sailing and the sea comes directly from him," a woman named Katie said.

"He didn't just teach us the ropes of the sea trade, he also taught us the lore of the sea, its stories, and history. I love the ocean and its ways because of him."

"We will carry on his legacy," another said.

"Your music was wonderful, Destiny," Katie said. "You have a real gift there." She smiled.

Pulling something out of her knapsack, Katie turned to Jessica and said: "Here, Jessica, we want you to have this. It is Hieronymus's personal banner which was specially made for him."

She handed a folded cloth to her. Jessica brought it to her face and smelled the fabric. Unfolding it, she spread the banner out on the deck. It showed a dark blue background with a crested moon and unsheathed sabre, and silver stars over a calm, moon and star-lit ocean, all hand stitched. She thanked the young women.

"Oh, thank you so much. I will treasure this always."

They sat in silence for a while, listening to the gentle lap of the water against the hull of the ship. The dead had been honoured. It was now time to help the wounded recover and for life to get back to normal.

Maximum Mischief limped home in his defeat. The *Nemesis* was badly damaged and Smarmy Smirker ordered makeshift repairs to be made to keep the vessel seaworthy.

"We will need to take shelter somewhere," Smirker told Mischief.

"We will not be welcome in Hilltopia."

Clotilda and Rankle tried to console Mischief. They competed with each other in getting Mischief's attention, hoping to gain some favour for themselves.

"We will be safe once we get back to the castle," Rankle said.

"Leave me," Mischief said curtly.

The full weight of the major defeat had not quite sunk in with Mischief. He felt numb and stayed in his cabin in shock. He tried not to think too much, hoping his instincts would guide him to his next move. Deep in his heart, though, he knew he was broken. The bold grab for power had failed terribly and now he had to find a way to pick up the pieces.

Posey Pete and her pirate ships had scattered, defeated. They headed back to Little Havoc, their tails between their legs. Sick to the stomach, he tried to work out what went wrong. Was Buttondrop merely a superior opponent? Did he underestimate the forces gathered against him? He wracked his brain to find the reason for his failure, without success. He continued tearing at himself. Nothing was going to make him feel any better. He slumped into his chair in despair.

Clotilda joined Rankle on the deck. She held on to the ship's rail and looked out at the open sea.

"What will happen to us?" she said.

"I don't know. We have to wait and see. Master will figure it out, I'm sure," he said. They both chuckled, hideously.

News of the great naval victory soon reached all parts of the map. Reports trickled in from different sources – returning ships, the carrier pigeon network, visitors from Angarrad. There was much discussion about this great event.

In Hilltopia, the triumphant supply ships and their crews regaled the townsfolk with stories of valour and derring-do at the great sea battle. Public celebrations were planned by the town authorities. The Crumpled Faced People invited many Hilltopians to their sacred island for a huge celebratory feast. When the *Santa Rosa* made berth, crowds thronged the harbour foreshore hoping to get a glimpse of Buttondrop and the heroes as they came ashore. Cheers and much merriment met the companions who were a little overwhelmed by all the attention.

In Hermanstock, military bands played in the streets and the locals put on their finest clothes to attend the celebrations. Horses and carriages and single riders mixed with those on foot as children carried balloons and everyone had a smile on their face.

Buttondrop and the gang made their way to Angelique's property as their first order of business to view her newly rebuilt house. The devastation of losing her home had hit Angelique hard and she struggled to keep her head up in the face of all the hatred directed at her. In her mind's eye, she could still picture the fire that engulfed the property and the mad panic to keep everyone safe. The chance to rebuild comforted her despite the loss.

Angelique's friends had been busy gathering furniture and redecorating the inside of the home and Angelique was delighted to find that all her animals had been returned and put in their new quarters. Destiny and Shonky explored the premises, upstairs and downstairs, laughing and joking as they made their discoveries.

"Home. How good is it to be home? A new beginning," Angelique sighed.

Count Dabacus paid his respects and departed the jolly gathering with his crew. He was off to find out what happened to the *Glorious* after she was set adrift by Maximum Mischief. He had a few leads but was apprehensive about her fate. She was a sturdy boat and he thought she would have withstood any bad weather while adrift. He would check Angarrad for any reports of an abandoned boat. He would also enlist the help of seagoing ships from Hermanstock and Hilltopia in the search for his beloved *Glorious*.

As the sun dipped low in the sky, visitors left one by one after ensuring that Angelique was settled in her new home. Jack and Manky escorted some of them to their own homes, remembering to thank all on Angelique's behalf for their caring and consideration.

After a light dinner, the companions retired to the drawing room and made themselves comfortable. They regaled each other with many stories and anecdotes about their adventures. They laughed heartily but there were tears too for the fallen and all who had sacrificed their lives to protect them. At times, they would just sit in silence, each remembering for themselves what had happened to them. They would never forget.

Buttondrop went up to Destiny, smiling.

"It's time," he said.

The friends gathered around her, chatting excitedly.

Jessica was first and gave Destiny a huge hug. Wiping away a tear, she told her that she had made a wonderful friend and that she would never forget her. They held each other tightly.

Manky came up and touched her nose playfully.

"Angelique has the dolphin I carved for you and will put it in a special place for your return," he said.

"Oh Shonky, what a time you've been through! There is never a dull moment when you are around, that's for sure," she laughed. They embraced.

Angelique approached, smiling gently. She looked fondly into Destiny's eyes and took her in her arms. They didn't say anything to each other. They had a quiet but full understanding between them.

They all proceeded to Destiny's bedroom. Jessica pulled down the bed covers and fluffed up the pillows.

Destiny climbed in. Silently, Jack approached and lifted Destiny's hand. He put the coral ring he had fashioned on her finger. She smiled and said nothing.

Buttondrop stepped forward and touched Destiny on the head.

"You have been through a great adventure with us," he said.

"You may not remember it all at once when you get home but bits and pieces will fall into place and make happy memories for you. Some sad, too.

"You told me you were okay with the adoption by your foster carers. Good. They will love you dearly and take care of you. This is not goodbye, remember sweet Destiny, this is farewell, we will meet again. Safe passage home."

Tears and smiles filled the room as everyone focused on sending Destiny home. The trials and dangers of their experience helped them bond even more closely with each other. They began to sing, gently, as Destiny closed her eyes and dozed off.

THE ADOPTION PARTY

"This is the big day! Wake up, silly," Sarah said, as she rustled Destiny in her bed. Sarah was Destiny's best friend and they shared everything together. Joined at the hip, foster mother Anita would quip.

Destiny yawned and looked around her. Yes, home again – Sparkles the cat was curled up on the end of the bed, all her things were in their right place, and she could smell the lavender infuser that gently filled the air with its perfume. *I'm in my bed,* she realised. *I must have crawled back in without even thinking.* She recalled having fallen asleep in her wheelchair. *Silly me,* she thought.

"Where did you get that?" Sarah said excitedly, pointing to the ring on Destiny's finger.

"Oh, from a toy dispenser at the local store," she said, trying not to look Sarah in the eye.

She felt puzzled – how on earth did that get there? She wondered at the magic that could make it happen. At first, she was a little taken aback, and afraid. Flashes of her dreams came back, a piece at a time, snapshots of her adventure. Destiny was a bit dazed and confused and looked around her room hoping something would bring her back down to earth.

A face appeared in her mind's eye – Hieronymus! *Oh,* she thought. Memories of his death came flooding back. A small tear formed in her eye. She turned away from Sarah so as not to let her see.

What had she learned from all her dream adventures? She thought of all the wonderful people she knew who loved and cared for her. Destiny felt a bit more grown up – she realised how much she loved all these people.

Her thoughts wandered to her parents. *Would they be proud of me? I have experienced so much recently, and been through so much*, she thought. *Have I let them down now that Anita and Anne will be my mums?*

A gentle calm descended on her.

Yes! she exclaimed to herself. *I can do this!*

She turned her attention back to Sarah who chatted excitedly.

"Come on, get dressed, we have to get this party started!" Sarah said. The pair went to the kitchen where Destiny's foster mother Anita busied herself preparing treats for the party.

"Good morning darling, did you sleep well?" Anita said. "I have laid out your party dress for the big event." She smiled warmly. "Sarah has been here for a while, waiting for you to wake up."

"I heard a few bumps coming from your room last night. Is everything all right?" she said.

"Yes, that was just Sparkles up to his tricks. I was trying to settle him down. I had these dreams," Destiny said. "A great adventure."

"Tell me later," Sarah said. "We have to go over the invitation list to see who's coming. This is your big day, your big adoption party day and we don't want anything to go wrong."

Grandmother Anne looked at her watch. "The music consultant should be here soon," she said.

Sarah and Destiny admired each other's party dresses. They both liked similar clothes. Destiny wore a sleeveless, full-length white dress with a black sash around the waist and black, fabric flowers on the skirt. Sarah wore a simple knee-length, sleeveless purple dress tied at the shoulders with ribbons. The girls wore matching shoes to complement their outfits.

The invited guests included children from Destiny's school and also from her social club which catered to young people in wheelchairs and with disabilities. Her local swimming club friends and mates from her music club were also invited.

Anne had organised a music appreciation party for the mothers and carers while the children were enjoying themselves. Guests were allowed to bring a pet if they wanted to and Destiny stipulated in the invitations that no one bring presents and flowers for her. If they wanted to do something special, they could make a donation to Destiny's favourite charity.

The first guest to arrive was Peter Robinson, with his pet green budgerigar Thomas.

"Thanks so much for coming, Peter. Do you want to put Thomas somewhere?" Destiny said. "Sarah, would you help Peter with his wheelchair? Thanks."

Peter had painted, coloured spokes on his wheelchair and all manner of ornaments draped over his chariot. It was a sight to behold and Destiny marvelled at his sense of fun.

"If it's okay he likes to perch on my shoulder. He won't fly around," Peter replied.

"Sure, make Thomas feel right at home," Destiny said with a smile.

Slowly, one by one, Destiny's party guests filled up the front room where balloons, streamers and other decorations got everyone into the party spirit. Once everyone had arrived, all the children were taken into the dining room where a long, large wooden table was filled with a riot of treats. Mums and carers stayed in the front room where a display of musical instruments was laid out.

The table was filled with trays of celery and carrot sticks with cream cheese dips, fairy bread glittering with hundreds and thousands, a huge cake with Destiny written in cream on the top, party pies, sausage rolls, low sugar cakes and lollies, and many other delights including a wide variety of fresh fruit. Jugs of flavoured drinks were placed among the goodies. Sarah had chosen the music and the sound of current favourite songs and artists filled the room. Everyone was having a good time.

"You had better slow down, Karen, you'll make yourself sick eating so fast!" Sarah said to one young girl.

"You wish, jellyfish," Karen said right back.

Sarah and Destiny giggled.

"No danger, park ranger!" someone yelled out.

"No drama, cane farmer!" yelled another.

This set off a chain reaction among the children.

"Hang loose, papa goose."

"Far out, brussel sprout."

"Up your nose with a rubber hose."

"If you don't risk it, you won't get the biscuit."

The room was in uproar with laughing children which drew the attention of the parents.

"What on earth is going on!" Anita exclaimed.

"Kids' fun, Mum," Destiny reassured her.

Satisfied that the children weren't getting into mischief, Anne took the mums and carers on a tour of the house to show them what they had done to make their home more comfortable for Destiny in her wheelchair.

"We widened all the doorways and put in French doors which are much more practical," she said.

Anne showed them the ramps, rails and handles peppered throughout the house, and the lowered toilet and bathroom sink which gave Destiny better access.

"I like the uncluttered feel of your home," one mum said. "There's plenty of turnaround room for the young one in her chair."

"Yes, and the lighting is great," another said.

Anne beamed.

A knock at the front door drew Anita away from the gathering. Destiny craned her neck from where she was sitting in the dining room to see if she could find out who was at the door. Whoever it was, they were ushered into the study without a fuss.

Anita came to the dining room.

"Children, I am just going to steal Destiny away from you for one moment. She won't be long, I promise."

Anita wheeled Destiny to her room and closed the door for privacy.

"Destiny, I have a very big surprise for you but first I want to prepare you," she said.

She sat on Destiny's bed and drew the young girl close to her.

"You have a brother and he is here to meet you," Anita said bluntly.

"I have a brother?" Destiny cried.

"Yes. He is the son of your father. When your father was a young man, he had a short relationship with a young woman and a boy was born. His name is Aloysius and he has come here to meet you. Now, the decision is wholly yours. He has already accepted if you don't want to meet him. He understands it could be very painful for you. Take a moment to think quietly about your decision," Anita said.

After a brief moment, Destiny smiled at Anita.

"Yes, I want to meet him," she said.

Entering the study, Destiny found a tall, lanky young man in cowboy boots, jeans, belt and a checkered shirt holding a black cowboy hat with a small coloured feather in the side. He looked nervous. Destiny's face lit up.

"Hello Destiny, I am Al, your older brother," he said.

She held out her hand.

"Pleased to meet you, Al."

"It's a very special day for you. I'm glad I could make your celebration. Here, I have brought you these," he said as he produced a bunch of multi-coloured carnation flowers, an apple pie, and a video of the movie *Grease.*

"Oh, thank you," she said. "I don't know this movie – what is it about?"

"Lots of singing and dancing, lots of fun," Al grinned.

"Wow! You know Mum and Gran. Come and meet my other friends," Destiny said.

"That would be nice, thank you," Al said.

Back at the party, Destiny got everyone's attention with a whistle.

"Gang, I want you to meet my brother, Al," she said proudly.

"Hello Al," they all sang in unison.

"I know who you are!" Peter Robinson cried out.

"Who might I be?" Al said, amused.

"A V.I.B.," he said.

"What's a V.I.B.," Al said, frowning.

"A Very Important Boy!" Peter laughed.

The other children pointed and laughed.

"Okay," Al said, raising his eyebrows.

Gathering in the front room, the adults and children were treated to a jam session with Destiny's mates from the music club. They had all brought their instruments and Destiny, on clarinet, led the musical treat. There were trumpets, saxophones, violins and a whole array of classical instruments which the children teased and coaxed creating a wonderful sound. Everyone in the room clapped along in appreciation.

The afternoon went quickly and soon it was time for the guests to leave. Mums and carers fussed over their charges and readied them for departure. Taking a position at the front door, with Al at her side, Destiny told them one last thing.

"Most parties have the guests giving presents to the person the party is being held for but this time it will be different. You will all get a small something from me and my family to remember my special day, my adoption day," she said.

As the children shuffled along, Destiny gave each a small medallion of St Christopher, the patron saint of travellers. Everyone smiled in surprise and appreciation. As the last ones filed out, Anita and Anne set about cleaning up the party mess.

"Go out onto the verandah, you two, you need time together to talk," Anne said to Destiny and Al. "We'll be busy here for quite some time, I imagine."

Destiny wheeled herself outside as Al followed.

The sun was low in the sky as they talked to each other about their lives, their dreams and their ambitions.

"I work on a cattle station out west," he told her.

"Do you work with horses?" Destiny said excitedly, "I love horses!"

"Yes. We use them in our work."

"There's not much to tell about me," Destiny said, "but I have the most amazing dreams. Want to hear about them?" she ventured.

"Yes," Al said, curious.

"Well, let me see, there's Buttondrop and Angelique. He is the Wish-Master and she is the Dream Guardian. There's Manky and Shonky, the twin boys who are always getting into trouble. There is Jack, who rescued me from Maximum Mischief's prison, and Count Dabacus with his magic. We have just been at sea, a mighty sea battle and ..."

"Whoa, Destiny, slow down. Wow, this sounds amazing. All in your dreams, you say? Don't tell me all at once, I want to hear all the details. We will see each other much more now so you can tell me a little bit every time we meet. Okay? Is that okay?"

"Yes, I would like that," she said.

Al then did something unexpected. He picked Destiny up from her wheelchair and held her in his arms.

"Let's watch the sun go down together. I love the colours of the sunset," he said.

She wrapped her arms around his neck and rested her head on his shoulder. They were quiet. The great journey had come to a close but not quite the way Destiny expected. The shock of finding her long-lost brother would take a while to sink in but there was plenty of time. Her mind wandered back to the sea in all its grandeur and adventure. She would have some great stories to tell Al. Right now, everything was perfect. She closed her eyes, content.

THE END

Acknowledgments

A heartfelt thanks to the following people who were so helpful in getting this project off the ground:

The late Dave Letch whose valuable input into the manuscript will always bear his name; the late Viki Winterton whose work on launching the first book, *Destiny's Dream*, was significant; Pam Murphy who stepped up to the plate when Viki passed on; my mentor Edwina Shaw who gave me handy hints on presentation; Claudio Tinnirello for her vision with the website; the team at Pickawoowoo Publishing without whom none of this would have been possible; the great illustrator Christopher Brunton who has once again captured the spirit of the story in pictures; and last but not least my good friend and healer Riccardo Caniato who spurs me on to creativity when the road gets dark. And finally, Eddie Albrecht, my editor at Pickawoowoo who has polished my words into something magical.

Thanks, one and all, may your stories go with you wherever you travel.